Both Fingers Crossed

Cover design by Ashley Santoro
ISBN (paperback) 979-8-9863881-7-5
ISBN (ebook) 979-8-9863881-6-8
ISBN (audiobook) 979-8-9863881-8-2

Water's Edge Publishing LLC
waters.edge.publishing@gmail.com

Both Fingers Crossed

Montgomery Brothers, Book 3

Anna Alkire

WATER'S EDGE PUBLISHING

CHAPTER ONE

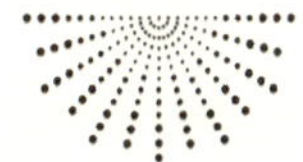

Maggie's phone rattled, buzzing with distorted beeps. The cracked screen read "Scumbag Lawyer." She crossed her fingers and knocked on her gran's old wooden breakfast table.

"Hi, Mr. Filch, this is Maggie."

He grunted deep in his throat. "Sweet girl, I have news. The estate is out of probate. Your grandmother's trailer is yours if you make the debt payments. Come on down to my office tonight, after six. We'll work out an arrangement. As you know, there's the little matter of my fee—"

Maggie made static noises with her mouth, turning on the kitchen fan and putting her face next to the whirring blades. "Mr. Filch," she shouted, "I'm driving through a tunnel, I didn't make out any of that. What did you say?"

"What tunnel? Get your ass down to my office or—"

"Oh, my goodness, I'm so sorry, I can't hear a word you're saying. And my phone's going to die any second. Don't you worry, Mr. Filch, I'll be sending payment just as quick as a cricket."

"Maggie Soloski, you better—"

Her phone died. She slumped against the kitchen counter, kissing her Djucu-nut necklace. Her luck would turn around, she knew it. In the meantime, she wouldn't be home during the day for a while. The old lecher would try to catch her outside her trailer.

Toto stared up at her, his ears pricked. "Leash. Fetch." Tongue hanging out, Toto cocked his head, his small black eyes darting over to the bench by the door. He took off, limping a little on his bad back leg. Ten seconds later he dropped the leash at her feet. Maggie fed him a piece of hot dog.

She pulled on her big jacket. How could that man call her on a Sunday before church? She huffed. He had her over a barrel, that's how. She snatched up the paper plate holding her homemade cream horns then walked out the door. By hook or by crook, she had to come up with the money to pay his lawyer fees.

Her old minivan spluttered to life. She stared at the yellow and brown trailer she'd inherited from her gran along with a pile of debt. All kinds of people had told her to walk away. The truth was, it was all she had left.

At church, old Ms. Hazel smiled at her and shuffled over. "Maggie, what have you brought for us today?" She was taking her turn greeting the small congregation that showed up for service at Ridgeview Presbyterian. "Don't tell anyone, but your treats are my favorite part of Sunday."

Maggie winked at her. "They're called lady locks in Pittsburgh. Here in Idaho, better known as cream horns." She took the plastic covering off the plate to let the puff pastry breathe. She'd had to use old flour and cheap shortening instead of butter. At least her pantry wasn't completely bare. *Yet.*

"Oh my, don't those look good." Ms. Hazel clapped her hands together.

Maggie's mouth quirked up. She was so grateful for the little group of women at church, even if she didn't know how to tell them. They'd become the only thing like family she had left.

"Dear," Ms. Hazel said, glancing around at the mostly empty lobby room. "Your friends here, myself included, have wanted to do something for you during your hard time. It isn't much, just a hundred dollars, but we'll be giving it to you during the coffee hour. I wanted you to know, so you aren't surprised."

Maggie put the plate down on the entryway table and hugged her. "You didn't need to do that. I'm going to be fine." She pulled away quickly, looking down to adjust her bag while her eyes stung. If the ladies knew what she was planning, they wouldn't be fundraising for her.

"Of course you are, dear." Ms. Hazel patted her shoulder. "You're only paying for your grandmother's sins. The damn twit."

Maggie snorted. "Gran wasn't any good with money."

"Left you with enough debt to pay for culinary school, twice over. Are you finally going to sell that trailer?"

Maggie glanced up at the stained glass window above the big oak entry doors. Her monthly payments toward the debt were more than she'd pay in rent for a cheap apartment, but at least she owned the dang trailer.

The problem was, there wasn't anything for her in Ridgeview, Idaho. She had to get out. "I'm thinking it's time for me to move. Go to Nevada for school."

Ms. Hazel nodded, oblivious to what Maggie was really planning. "Go for it, dear. We'll miss you though."

After the service and coffee hour, Maggie left her minivan in the church parking lot and walked down the oak-lined streets of downtown Ridgeview. Toto pranced next to her on his leash, wearing his red plaid sweater.

Most of the big old houses in that neighborhood had Christmas lights along every ridge of their roofs and garlands of evergreen and red ribbon wrapping their front porches. She stuffed her hands in her pockets. Her ex-boyfriend's parents' beautiful three-story was one block over. Well, her most significant ex-boyfriend. She'd dated too many dang people in that little town.

Her breath huffed out in white bursts. Nevada would be warmer than Idaho. Her plan made the hairs on the back of her neck stand up but she had to do something. *I'm cold enough.* Inside she'd been frozen for years. She turned around and walked back to her minivan.

A familiar black sedan blasting heavy metal took the turn into the parking lot, going fast. Toto barked. She picked the little terrier up and held him against her chest.

Maggie's stomach clenched into a tight ball. Her best friend, Andy, slammed on the breaks, skidding the back wheels around forty-five degrees and stopping feet from where she stood.

He sat in the car staring at her, window rolled down, for a full thirty seconds. There were bags under his eyes, easy to see on his pale freckled skin underneath the shag of dyed black hair. Andy had been her best friend since he'd thrown a punch for her in middle school.

Ten days ago, he'd pinned her down and forced a hard kiss on her. Then he'd cried and tried to keep her from leaving. She'd ignored his phone calls ever since.

The truck door creaked open. Maggie took a deep breath. His brown eyes raked over her face. She didn't know what to say to him.

"Why the hell haven't you called me back?" Andy pushed his hair out of his eyes, his body shivering in the cold. He only ever wore T-shirts, probably to show off his tattoo sleeves. He crouched low to light a cigarette.

Maggie put Toto down. She shoved her hand in her jacket pocket and pulled out her keys. "It's too cold out here to talk. I'll call you when I'm ready."

Andy sprung back up, blowing smoke sideways. "We have to talk, Mags. I can't stop thinking about what happened. Damn, it's cold—can we sit inside my car?"

"No."

"Seriously?"

"Go warm up. I'm headed to the diner to pull an extra shift. Marlene is slammed and—"

"Wait, just listen to me." He flung down his cigarette and put an arm out, partially blocking her way. Toto growled then walked forward and sniffed his shoes. "I love you, Mags —you sure as shit know that." He swung away from her and stared out at the busy road nearby. Hands in his pockets, he glared over his shoulder at her. "We've been together but not together for years, the only couple in town that doesn't fuck. Instead, I have to watch you jump from asshole to asshole while I pick up the pieces."

"Wow. You're wound up tighter than a tick." She put Toto inside the minivan. "I thought we were friends," she said, staring at the four-leaf clover stuffy hanging from her rearview mirror. "What you did was wrong, and you know it. You need consent. Promise me you won't do that again, to anyone."

"Fuck. Yeah—I promise."

With her back to Andy, she closed her eyes, taking a deep breath. To be honest, she'd considered sleeping with him a few times, knowing on some level how much he wanted it. It wouldn't be bad. He smelled like his deodorant and kept himself tidy. He wasn't ugly, especially his big brown eyes. Skinny and awkward but not in a bad way. The problem was she didn't want him like that—and felt sick contemplating what would happen after. Leading him on at all would end their friendship. But it looked like he was ending their friendship anyway.

"Why not me, Maggie?" She turned around to watch him pace on the asphalt. His pale skin was flushed bright red. "We're best friends so why the hell not me?"

"I'm leaving." The words came out of her mouth and fell through the air like stones. "I'm moving to Vegas to…" She swallowed. "Go to school."

"What?"

"You heard me. I've got to go—try to get a better job." Maggie clasped the Djucu nut on her necklace. "Culinary school. It's there, and I have to get started."

"Wait, you don't have any money—the funeral, the lawyer fees for probate or whatever, paying all the medical bills. Toto needs that damn surgery on his leg. You told me you were broke and that the minivan was barely running!"

"Hey, don't talk about Mini-V like that. She's sitting right there and can hear you."

"Oh my God, just hold on. Hold the fuck on."

It all came down to money. When a small town dropped you into the dirty receptacle that was trash, it was like the folds of the plastic bag pinned you to the bottom of the can. She'd grown up in a trailer with her grandmother. That was enough for public opinion. It didn't matter that she worked hard and did her best to be a good person. Her debt, her piss-poor job, and the trailer that still smelled like granny's cigarettes were about to zombie-chomp the life right out of her. Men saw her in one kind of way—even her best friend. Maybe she could do something about it.

Maggie squeezed her crossed arms tighter against her chest. "I'm leaving," she repeated, dread clawing over her skin. *No turning back now.*

"What are you going to do? Where are you going to stay?"

She didn't answer. He stared at her, waiting. Then his

eyes opened wider, and his mouth dropped open. "Maggie. You can't drive to Vegas and sleep in your car—what if some asshole puts his hands on you?"

"I get that all the time around here."

"Mags, you know I'd never hurt you! Look, just calm down and think about this."

Maggie huffed. Andy was hyper-sensitive, hyper-emotional, hyper-energetic. She was like the pole that kept his whirling tetherball of energy from spinning off and getting lost. There had been this idea in her head, apparently fantasy, that they'd always be together as brother and sister. She loved him. He stalked over to his truck and grabbed another cigarette from the interior, mumbling to himself. He needed time to rein in his spinning hamster wheel of emotions.

Gran was gone. It still didn't seem real, even after a year. There wasn't anyone for Maggie to take care of anymore. And no one would know what she was going to do. Her life had been on hold for so long. She had to go, now, before she changed her mind.

Rain started plopping down on her head. Maggie cleared her throat. "I'm going to Vegas to try—to see what happens."

ONE WEEK LATER, Maggie pulled down on the skirt of her apron, the cold air on her bare butt cheeks raising goose bumps all over her skin. Everyone was in a thong or less. She could have worn bunny slippers with her sexy housewife getup and been comfortable, but instead four-inch-high-heeled Mary Janes pinched her toes. Her shoes were modest compared to the other women waiting to interview at The Dirty Rabbit Ranch brothel.

The woman behind her tapped her foot on the white marble floor of the big lobby. "They're late," she muttered.

Two hours of standing in a line, in costume, had hammered in several points. First, there were forty-seven other people, mostly women, leaning against the walls or holding a place in the main line for the audition. There was stiff competition and a lot of it. Second, they were all valued about as much as cattle. And third, second-guessing herself was churning up the acid in her stomach. Fourth, if an energy bar would materialize in her bag she'd really appreciate it. *Probably won't get the job anyway.*

A young guy with a huge camera strolled around asking to take pictures. Maggie said no. Then she repeated herself and pushed his lens away. Bile burned a hole in her side. What if someone found out she was doing this?

The front of the line cheered as the double doors in front of them opened. Standing on her toes and craning sideways she could make out the open space beyond the doors, a large main room for the "resort." There was a long table set up in the middle of the big room with two people sitting behind it. A big bald man and a grim-faced woman stared at them with unsmiling faces.

The first person in line answered questions in a high giggly voice and slowly turned to show her backside. The man, red-faced with a deep orange tan that glistened on his bald head, sneered and rubbed his leg under the table. Maggie swallowed hard. Her vision swam in and out of focus.

"Excuse me. Hey, I lost my place in line up ahead when I *had* to go piss. I'm jumping in right here in front of you."

Maggie swung her head around, groggily realizing she was the one being talked to. A cream-faced blonde glared back at her, her face ferret-like, her thin red lips puckered up. The blonde tilted her head in a what-are-you-going-to-do-about-it challenge. Petite and slender, she balanced on insanely high black stiletto boots, her hand on an aggressively cocked hip.

Maggie cleared her throat. She hadn't spoken in hours, too nervous to attempt small talk with anyone. "Well, I'm not going to fight you about it," she said. "My toes hurt too much."

The tall athletic woman behind Maggie, whose dark good looks resembled Serena Williams, snorted and grumbled something about a damn liar. She didn't move to make a scene though. Her toes probably hurt too.

Ferret girl flashed Maggie a tight smile and sashayed into place, her pink silky robe swishing. She immediately pulled out a compact from her leather bag and flipped it open, examining every inch of her face.

"Where did you get that sexy little apron?" she asked while reapplying lipstick. "The French-maid look is cliché but always hot."

"I made it." Her costume was more horny-housewife-serving-an-evening-cocktail than French maid. All black, with three flounces in the skirt that barely reached Maggie's upper thigh, the apron had delicate black lace around the low-cut square chest. A bright red silk peony flower was attached to the broad black ribbon at the waist. The little almost black dress wrapped up her figure like the fondant on a petit-four cake, beautiful icing that left the spongy body underneath to the imagination. It made her slightly less jittery and likely to puke to have an apron on, as opposed to the G-string and teddy that ferret girl wore under her open robe.

"I saw one of these bitches wearing sweatpants—can you believe that? So disgusting."

"It's honest anyway."

"Not for me. I'm going to blow all those sloppy whores out of the water." She flashed a toothy white grin.

"Uh-huh." Maggie pressed her fingertips into the back of her neck. They were at the doorway. "Not sure I can do this," she muttered. Her nerves tap-danced on her brain. She closed her eyes, the drying sweat on her skin clammy.

"You should take off those glasses," Ferret girl said.

Maggie blinked, her eyebrows raised. The glasses were props that she didn't actually need, with plastic blue-screen lenses. They were also a halfhearted disguise in case someone took her picture.

Ferret girl flicked her blonde hair and rolled her eyes. "I'm serious. Take off the glasses. You'll almost look like a watered-down Marilyn Monroe without those ugly things on."

"If I take the glasses off, they might realize my superhero identity," Maggie said. The tall woman behind her snorted.

They stepped forward into the large room. She could sense the old potato head's eyes on her. The bottom of her stomach bounced around on the carpet under her Mary Jane heels. With a gut-twisting effort, she plastered a smile on her face. A song blasted from the speaker next to them, the base vibrating the apron ruffles on her thighs.

"Let's dance!" Ferret girl grabbed Maggie's hips and ground against her, forcefully rocking to the beat. Maggie froze then flinched from a hard pinch on her hip. Ferret girl gave her a come-on-stupid look, her eyebrows pushed up as high as they could go.

Like a robot with squeaky hinges, Maggie raised her arms above her head and moved her shoulders in counterpoint to her hips. Ferret girl grinned and grabbed the glasses off Maggie's face. She slithered down the black apron, turning around as she came up to push her backside against Maggie's groin. It was like getting a lap dance in the supermarket line, except everyone was wearing lingerie. Maggie blinked; she hadn't slept much the last two nights and nothing seemed altogether real.

Ferret girl sprang away and giggled, putting an arm around Maggie's waist. "There," she said in Maggie's ear, "that got the old dick's attention. I just got you a job."

~

THE NEXT DAY, Maggie stared at the desk with a public computer on it, in the corner of the main room at the brothel. She had to get over there. She edged away from the group of women surrounding a couple of truckers who wanted to "party." Party was the big euphemism around The Dirty Rabbit Ranch.

During a stay at the Dirty Rabbit, you could get a bubble bath, hot oil massage, a triple-decker bacon burger, or a couple's suite hotel room. The decor was warm neutrals with pops of gold, in cheaply done Egyptian style. The main service, though, was a legal sex worker of your choice. Maggie shivered, even though the room was warm.

She worked at a legal brothel. After her interview yesterday, she'd been offered a spot at the Dirty Rabbit. In her head she'd pictured a scene a bit like speed dating, or a raunchy party where the guy tried to kiss you the first time you danced with him. At the brothel, there hadn't been a man through the door yet that was even close to her age. It was nothing like she'd imagined, and she'd made the biggest mistake of her life.

She eyed a bowl of peanuts on the bar. Her stomach growled but she couldn't make her hands move. Technically, she had found out, she was an independent contractor. That meant that she actually paid the brothel to be there, forty-six dollars a night. They took half of whatever she made, and she paid for all her expenses. Including a hundred-dollar doctor exam once a week that she had gotten through yesterday after the audition. Her gift from the church ladies had covered that bill, sadly. After all was said and done, she'd blown through her entire budget and was now dead broke. That last paycheck from the diner in Idaho had burned up when she'd had to put a new starter in the minivan so that she could actually drive to Nevada. She wasn't going to make a cent working unless she slept with someone.

Maggie realized she was rubbing her arms and made herself stop. *Culinary school, pastry chef.* Her chest was so tight. The walls of the room were closing in on her. Her emotions had switched on this morning, examined what she was doing, and said *absolutely not, you stupid impulsive idiot.* Someone cackled and she startled.

Ferret girl had decided to call herself Princess. She walked into the room, a large glass of wine in hand, back from her first "party." She sidled up to Maggie and put her head on her shoulder. She smelled like perfume and mouthwash.

"Damn, I just made a hundred dollars an hour."

"You okay?" Maggie said.

"Fine. Politest fuck I've ever had."

Maggie let out a shaky sigh. Could she get on that damn computer for ten minutes? The computer was for the girls to promote themselves and contact clients online, with usage monitored. Phones were banned on the working floor and there was no free Wi-Fi. The female manager, with eyes like a hungry vulture, watched them all.

"What's wrong with you? You're all stiff. And sweaty too. Oh my God, put some powder on that nose. Jeezus." Princess scanned her with her face wrinkled up in a frown. "You're not being stupid and getting cold feet, are you?"

"I'm, uh, having a panic attack. No big." Maggie's heart

raced in her chest like a rabbit two seconds ahead of bloody fangs.

"Take a pill," Princess whispered angrily. "I keep telling you."

An apple-shaped man walked their way, his eyes running up and down Maggie, then lingering on her cleavage above the apron top. She plastered a smile on her face and said to Princess, "My tummy is a little messed up. I'll be back when it's, um, cleared up."

"Ugh, you're disgusting."

She hightailed it away from the potential client and back to her room. Actually refusing a client to their face, without an explanation other than, "I can't do it," could be enough to make the client leave the brothel altogether. And get her kicked out for the night.

She took a deep breath and stared at her tight face in the mirror of her bathroom. She wanted to check on Toto, hopefully burrowed under his sleeping bag. Winter in the Mojave Desert was about twenty degrees warmer than Idaho but forty degrees was still cold. Her van didn't have a working heater. *Culinary school. Pastry chef.* Her stomach growled. She had to think rationally. *I need more gas,* was all she could come up with.

An hour later, someone banged on her door. Maggie covered her face with her arm. Bang bang bang.

"Maggie," came a muffled shout. "It's Princess. Open the damn door."

After wiping her face with the heels of her hands, Maggie got up and unlatched the door. Princess bustled in holding two shot glasses, limes, and a saltshaker.

"Saltine crackers and ginger ale?" Maggie put a hand over her roiling mid-section.

Princess clanged everything down on a table. "Money!

Think of the damn money. Don't you at least want to make back what you spent here?"

"What's it to you? You'll have another designer handbag by midnight." Maggie took a small taste of the tequila and shuddered.

"You're being stupid—and that manager asked me where you were. You'd better get your tail out there and show your face."

She swallowed another sip of the liquor and sucked on a lime. "I'm thinking about some french fries. You hungry?"

"Fine. Get your ass up and shake out that hair. Gawd, you should pay me pimp fees."

Before they could order food, a bell rang and a lineup was called out in the lobby. Princess nodded and marched out with the rest of the girls. Maggie bent over to adjust her heel and then scurried out of the room, into a hallway bathroom. She hid in there with the door cracked, waiting until the great room was empty.

With her heels in her hands so they didn't click on the floor, she crept across the carpet to finally sit in front of the computer. Her fingers flew over the keyboard opening multiple browser windows, searching for food-service job openings in Vegas. She took a picture of the screen with her phone she'd snuck in, not wanting to waste time with paper. She looked down at the picture—blurry. *Damn it.*

Someone cleared their throat behind her. Maggie whipped around to see the hard-eyed manager staring at her. Quickly, she closed everything down on the computer and then stood up.

"You weren't in the line," said the manager in a cold voice.

"Oh sorry. I've been having some stomach problems and had to run to the bathroom."

Steely gray eyes bored into her brain, no doubt analyzing every weakness. "If you want to finish out the night here, you'll come to the next lineup." She patted her curly bottle-red hair. "And that computer is for industry-related business only. Have I made myself clear?"

"Yes ma'am," said Maggie.

The bell rang again.

CHAPTER TWO

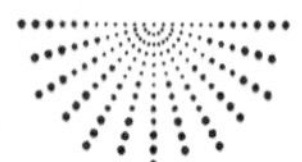

Chase slammed his hammer into the old drywall, cracking it open like a boiled egg. Demolition soothed the beast inside him. Sweat ran down the back of his neck. Gutting the piece-of-shit ranch from the seventies that had sat vacant for at least a year, after a lifetime of abuse and neglect, was a service to the city of Las Vegas. Broken pieces of drywall piled up around his feet while he stripped it back to the studs.

His crew would put in another two hours and get the demo done tonight, if they wanted to keep their jobs. He moved into the kitchen to tear down the dark, warped cabinets. He'd bought the little Tulle Springs ranch at auction, and he wanted to flip it fast. Owning two flip houses was a risk.

"Dang, boss," said Jose, emerging from the main bathroom covered in dust. "You're kicking ass, huh?"

Chase grunted. "Tell those lard-asses outside to haul this shit to the dumpster."

"Boss, it's five o'clock. This day is squeezing my balls." Jose cracked open a beer can. Chase stopped and watched him wipe his face with a handkerchief. "We've been here since seven this morning."

Dumping half a water bottle down his throat didn't cool his temper. "We're still here so we don't have to come back tomorrow. What the fuck is wrong?"

Jose crossed his arms. "I only got tonight to get happy. Tomorrow, I go to Maria's family, even though she broke up with me, and that's it for my weekend. Johnny is all jumpy. Ben's in his head. If we don't do something, we're gonna be angry pieces of shit."

Chase was already there, and had been for a long time. It had been months since he'd had his cock in anything besides his hand. He'd been thinking about a trip over to Pahrump for a while. An hour's drive and a whole resort full of women that wanted nothing from him but his money. But letting someone touch him could shatter the tenuous control he had on himself. And he was damn picky.

"You like workin' for me, Jose?"

"Damn, boss—what's the big deal? We be back on Monday…"

"No, Monday I'm workin' for Sandstone at the Summerlin job. They're hiring reliable contractors for big money that could actually pay for that shiny-ass new truck of yours. You walk now and I won't hire you for shit."

"Fuck man, calm down." Jose threw his empty can in a bin. He grabbed a bag of trash in each hand and headed out toward the dumpster. A minute later Mexican Banda music vibrated the floorboards, blasting from Jose's truck parked in the driveway. Chase shook his head.

The toddler crew went into tantrum mode. Everyone loves swinging around a sledgehammer for the first hour, then it becomes work. The cleanup at the end of the day might as well be called purgatory. He was so damn sick of being a hard-ass.

Not that he'd ever tell them, but he liked this crew. Even if helping out other army vets, recently out of the service, could be an emotional land mine. They needed to go, move, taste, live. The stupid irony was he was as bad as any of them. Maybe worse. Making money hid a truckload of problems.

The clang and thud of objects hitting the inside of a dumpster picked up out in the driveway. Chase sped up his own pace. Getting Jose, Johnny and Ben work was his nod to the future. That insubstantial ethereal place where he wanted to live. He wrenched a long rectangle of pressboard cabinet off the wall. It fell on the floor with a crack as its sides split apart. Dust from the exposed plywood subfloor swirled up, coating his jeans and T-shirt with another layer of grayish powder.

Whatever the future held, the present was dirty. He needed to work until he could pass out, his brain numbed with exhaustion. Somewhere there was a wall he wasn't going to be able to break through, where working and drinking didn't keep him moving any longer. *Not today, soldier.* He swung the hammer again.

"Dude, look at the ass on her." Johnny limped in, his small wiry frame moving fast despite the prosthetic that had replaced half of his right leg. He held up a screen in front of Chase.

"Get that thing out of my face. Jesus, anything that's been in your back pocket needs a buffer zone." He pulled off his eye gear and wiped his face on the inside of his shirt. Soaked with sweat, his T-shirt smelled like his deodorant wore off about ten hours ago.

"Dude, that girl is an escort. She took this picture and sent it to me—says she's getting on her fucking pantyhose right now."

"Johnny, get your limp-ass dick back to work."

"This girl will meet us anywhere. Anywhere. Dude, let's

get out of here and fucking hop on this shit." Johnny was new to Vegas. The city would drain him as dry as a creosote bush in high summer.

Chase put his goggles back on. "You leave now and I won't hire you again."

"Dude, you need this more than I do. She's gonna be ready all night."

Chase threw the last cabinet across the room toward the pile of garbage. It hit an exposed beam instead, splitting it down the middle with a snap like a balloon popping. *Damn it all to hell.*

Johnny walked to the pile of warped pressboard and started chucking it all into a bin. "Ben ain't right, man. We've got to do something to help the poor bastard."

"Oh, you're mister altruistic now, usin' illegal prostitutes to help a friend. Right."

"Dude, he ain't said three words today. It's bad—you know."

Chase did know. Ben wasn't settling into civilian life at all, and the stress had him shaky and twitchy as hell.

"The boy needs a blow job," said Johnny. "Fucking miracle cure for anything."

"Thank you, Doctor Strangelove."

Jose whooped and salsaed across the doorway. Chase rolled his eyes. His guys were likely to get arrested. Prostitution was illegal in Clark County and seeking it out in Vegas was like playing against the house. The Johns got booked—especially easy targets like these naive cheap idiots. If they'd all just put their dicks away, they'd be done in less than an hour.

He glared out the back door and spotted Ben leaning against a corner of the house, sucking on a cigarette. His hand shook so hard his lips twitched against the short stub of burned-up filter he barely got into his mouth.

"Hey, Ben," Chase said, walking outside. "You don't have any cigarette left there, partner."

"Oh yeah…" Ben dropped the cigarette and put his hand over his face. His whole body shuddered.

Chase whistled. "Just hang in there. It's gonna pass. I know, I've been through it."

"I'm sorry, man. I shouldn't be here. It's just…" His voice trailed off. Chase waited. "I, um, I can't be alone right now."

"Yeah." Chase suppressed a sigh. "You're right." Shit, he would have to do something about this. "Grab that pile of wood and follow me." Together they hauled the old deck boards into the garage. He pretended not to notice Ben's wet eyes and muffled chokes.

The dumpster was stacked past the brim. Jose and Johnny had just settled a long piece of rotten carpet padding onto the top when they all realized Chase was staring at them.

"All right, assholes, here's the deal. We're driving to Pahrump and going to the Dirty Rabbit. It's legal, clean, and the first round of blow jobs is on me." Jose and Johnny cheered. "But nobody's going to see a single round ass until this job is as finished as a backward cowgirl squeezing my balls."

CHASE RANG the outdoor bell of The Dirty Rabbit Ranch. Tension churned low in his pelvis. His pulse trotted along, and he clenched his teeth.

"Dude," said Johnny, "it's freakin' cold."

The desert air was dry, the breeze dusty and tangy with creosote. Chase liked it out here in this part of the Mojave Desert. They were a good sixty miles away from the big city, in the middle of wide-open and deadly parched land.

Johnny and Jose jostled each other, voices too loud and

breathless as they pushed to be first through the door. Ben was pale, hunched over like a man on his way to an emergency colonoscopy. He wasn't even pretending not to be nervous. Chase scrubbed a hand over his face. They weren't going to prolong this. They'd have a lineup of the girls available and skip all the pussyfooting in the main room. In and out and fast, in so many ways.

The door opened. "Dude. This is awesome," Johnny said, swaggering into a wide vaulted entryway. The cream room had gold-framed nude paintings on the walls and a box store chandelier hanging from the ceiling. It was a bit nicer than the old western facade on the front of the building had led them to believe. The white marbled tile on the floor looked recently installed. Obviously, business at The Ranch turned a profit.

Women started clicking out from the main room, nearly all of them smiling and winking as they checked over Chase's crew. No doubt reasonably good-looking men, ready to spend money, were a welcome sight around here. Crossing his arms, he leaned against a wall, his face hard. He didn't want pity from anyone, especially a fake cuddle to make him feel better about being single and miserable. *Fuck that.*

A black apron with a red flower on it caught his eye. The comparatively modest garment was on a blonde with curly hair and a curvy figure. She wore bunny slippers and thick black glasses. Her backside flashed at him, uncovered behind the apron except for a skimpy thong. His cock hardened. *Damn.* She positioned herself behind a large potted tree. Was she trying to avoid being picked?

A cabbage-faced older woman grabbed her elbow and pulled her over into the line. All three of the other men pivoted her way. She stood out, her solemn pretty face turned away as she grabbed the necklace around her neck. Some part of him said, *No, that one's dangerous.* The rest of him twitched in approval. What the hell perverse part of him was turned on by a reluctant prostitute? She obviously didn't want to be there. Was it some kind of reverse psychology lure?

Ben stood up taller and took a step toward the blonde with the glasses. Chase moved before his brain could protest. He brushed past Ben and walked over to stand in front of the bunny slippers. Soft blonde curls framed her face and a pair of big turquoise eyes stared up at him through the cat-eye glasses. He held out his hand.

A sharp faced girl next to her nudged her arm. Slowly a cold hand settled into his. Absurdly, satisfaction crept over him.

He pulled her off to the side of the room. They stood in silence while Ben, Jose, and Johnny finished choosing. She was totally still. He could fall into that stillness, roll around in it like a dog on the beach. What was wrong with him?

He stared at her wide mouth, the lips full and pink. A hunk of thick blonde curl covered one side of her face. He resisted the urge to reach out and run his fingers through her hair. She seemed tough and vulnerable at the same time.

The rest of the room cleared out through a couple of double doors. She pulled her hand out of his.

"Um, what the h-e-double-toothpicks are you doing here?" she said.

He blinked and cocked his head. "You new here, babe?"

She blew a raspberry out of her mouth and pushed curls off her face. "All night it's been pasty-faced potbellied old flubbers. Then you walk in. Here's a news flash, you don't have to pay for it."

"You offerin' to step out with me?"

"Oh, no. Although you're attractive—the first guy I've…" She huffed, glancing sideways at the naked lady painting on the wall, then quickly away. Color rushed up into her cheeks.

"Right," she said, "I know, I'm dressed like a prostitute. I'm working in a brothel. But it's not for me." Abruptly her face tightened. She cleared her throat. "Please, pick one of the other girls," she said so quietly that he barely heard her. Her eyes darted up to him for only a second.

He was in one hell of a maudlin mood tonight because all he wanted to do was take her in his arms. "Are you here against your will?" he asked.

Her eyebrows and chin lifted then she shook her head slowly to each side. "Nope. My own stupid idea to make a buck. Um, thanks for asking." She blew out a breath. "As far as I can tell, none of the girls here are working against their will. There's a lot of regulation."

Her voice was low with a bit of warm rasp to it like she'd been slinging back bourbons. Somehow this unhappy girl had become the exact thing he wanted. His body revved like a diesel engine. Damn, he was fucked up. Another view of her backside and he'd be most of the way there.

"How about you let me pay you to come have a drink with me?" He gave in to the temptation to touch her hair. It was soft, the ends springing away from his fingers.

She didn't move. A sweep of thick eyelashes fanned out across her cheeks as burgundy flushed across her face. Her stomach made a huge growl, gurgling slowly back to silence.

"Shouldn't have eaten that bear yesterday," she mumbled. He felt himself grin a little, the underused muscles stretching tightly.

"All right," he said. "I'll up the ante. How about I pay you to let me buy you dinner?"

"At the sports bar next door?" She put her hands over her cheeks and peeped up at him through her lashes. "Okay."

"So, it's a date?" He stepped closer, reaching out to brush his fingers across the lace on her apron.

She took a deep breath. "I'm putting on jeans first."

She turned around and walked down the hallway, big black bow bouncing on the top of her high, heart-shaped ass as it clenched on either side of her thong. His breath caught and his balls ached.

~

With her free hand, Maggie touched her necklace. His hand was warm and large around hers, the inside rough with calluses. He'd insisted on holding her hand while they walked, his dark hazel eyes watching her face. He didn't smile. His thick eyebrows were a little pinched together, like he was concentrating on some dark internal thought.

Big muscles bunched and moved under his T-shirt. She was a little steamy—the man could have been the lead in a Hallmark movie, the single lumberjack in a small town, with a sad face and a dark past. It was the scruffy facial hair. He was the only man she'd seen that night that she'd actually been attracted to.

Being out of the strange brothel room, and wearing real clothes again, was letting her breathe. He put an arm around her waist as they waited in line at the sports bar on the brothel property. She leaned into him. There was a kind of intensity between them she hadn't really experienced before—or at least it seemed that way to her.

They ordered at the counter and got a couple of drinks. There were plenty of empty tables and he chose the one farthest away from the other people, tucked away in a dimmer corner. Kicking around the chairs, he positioned one against the wall then sat down, yanking on her hand and pulling her between his legs.

"Sit on my lap," he commanded in his deep growl.

"Um—okay."

He grabbed her hips and pulled her down onto one of his thighs. "I'm cold," he said, planting a dry kiss on her cheek.

She was stiff, but he sat there calmly and took a sip of his beer. It was a reminder that they weren't on a real date. He wasn't going to make small talk and ask about her hobbies. "I'm not a lap blanket," she grumbled.

"Nope, you're better." There was some country in his voice.

He picked up her soda and put the straw in her mouth, holding the glass while she took a couple sips. *What the heck?* Goose-bump-like prickles broke out on her skin. She'd never been involved with someone like him. He was obviously a control freak. Everything about him was so…masculine. His light brown hair was cut short, a grown-out buzz cut, and he had the bone structure to make it look good. His beard was barely grown in like he hadn't bothered to shave for a while. Somehow, though, it was all really working for her nether regions.

They stared at each other. His body was wide and hard with large shoulders and arms. And sweaty. His salty, malty, sharp pine and popcorn scent was all around her, like he'd come straight from work, only managing to splash clean and throw on a washed T-shirt. Maggie swallowed. She was getting hot all over.

Two burger baskets with fries were dropped in front of them, and three double whiskeys. He pushed one shot glass toward her and moved the baskets farther away. When she opened her mouth to protest, he plopped a fry inside. Distracted by the hot greasy food, she chewed, ravenous. He downed one of the doubles.

"What's with the withholding? Got an invalid's kink?" She reached for her basket, and he held it away from her. The man really was a devil—handsome and way too confident to be good. He brought up another fry in front of her mouth.

She let him slide it between her lips. "Watch out," she said, "a starving sex worker is dangerous."

"I have questions and I'm going to get answers," he said. He finished off the other whiskey.

"Fine. Then I want my food."

"Question one, why should I go with another girl tonight?"

He glared into her eyes. The urge to lean over and kiss him was toxically strong. Or at least run her hands through that ruff of thick hair. He was gorgeous and it had been a while. Or maybe it was thinking about sex all night, while everyone working pretended to be horny and turned on—or maybe they were—and then she'd miraculously ended up with him. She'd always been quick to jump when she was feeling it.

"You should go with another girl because I'm not a sure thing." Maggie thought there were flecks of green in his golden brown eyes, but it was hard to tell in the dim light. "I think you're here for something fast, not a first-timer who might bolt at any second."

He leaned back. She opened her mouth and he popped a fry inside.

"You're a sex worker that doesn't have sex?" he said, his eyebrows pinching together.

"Yeah, that's me. We're rare, but out there. I read it's big business in Japan." She opened her mouth. He delivered another fry.

"There are at least twenty-four women on the other side of this building who would put on a hospital gown if that's what you wanted." She propped her shoulder against the wall. "Why not hightail it over there and feed them french fries?"

Moving fast, he pressed his mouth against hers. A jolt of

lust rippled down her spine. She gasped and he cupped the back of her head, sliding his tongue between her slitted lips. *Holy hell.* He would be easy to sleep with. Except then she really would be a sex worker. *Think you're too good for this?* She was already disgusted with herself for being trashy enough to make out with a stranger in the corner of a grungy sports bar.

She pulled away, dragging in a jagged breath. Her heartbeat thudded in her ears. Light-headed, she held on to the edge of the table, blinking her eyes.

"I'm with you," he said, "because that's the only place my dick wants to be right now." He grabbed a fry and stuck it in his mouth.

She sniffed. *Not exactly romantic words.* "What about a massage?"

"No." He held up his empty glass at the bartender.

"Can I watch you take a bubble bath and do a little dance?" Did the man ever smile?

"No. But another time we'll start with that." He handed her the basket then leaned back, putting his head against the wall, watching her as she ate. "I'm not a relationship guy," he said.

Wow, big surprise. He must really have some baggage.

"In fact, I'm not good for women who...want an emotional attachment. But there's chemistry between us— that's rare. Let's go somewhere and enjoy it. I want to make you come until your eyes roll back in your head."

Maggie choked on a french fry. She reached out a shaky hand and took a sip of her soda.

"I will pay you very well to sleep with me," he said. His other hand gripped a fistful of her jeans and yanked her against his groin. His erection was rock hard. "And I'll be back soon to see you again."

"I won't be here," she said, squirming a little with the hot pressure of him under her. He was way more of a handful than she'd ever gone for.

He wrapped his arms around her. "No," he moaned and nuzzled the side of her neck.

The bartender dropped two more doubles on the table. He downed one fast. She managed a few more bites of her burger. Then his hands were sliding up the insides of her thighs. She swallowed a groan.

"Come work only for me," he mumbled in her ear, his breath hot and laced with liquor. "I'll pay a weekly rate."

He didn't seem real, his spiky eyelashes dark over his high cheekbones. She didn't even know his name. Could it be different—was it a real connection, would he want to date her if she wasn't a sex worker? *Not how this works.* He was wound up because she was teasing him, withholding, but still letting him have control. Actually, sleeping with him at the brothel would be safer than meeting him who knew where…

The door to the sports bar opened and a large group walked in with giggles and low laughs. Maggie saw the three men he had arrived with and Princess plus two of the other women who worked at the Dirty Rabbit.

"Chase," said a youngish man with a limp and a goatee. "Dude, you must have been fast."

Princess smiled, her hair rumpled and her lipstick smeared. She pounced on the chair next to Maggie, leaning over so she was snuggled into Chase.

Chase moved his chair away from Princess and positioned his body so that Maggie was completely between them, still on his lap. He didn't seem to notice Princess's sad pout face as he downed his other whiskey.

"Hey man," said the shy-looking guy with floppy black hair, "what's next on that house? When can we get back to work?"

"Shit man, he got all kinds of houses and projects," said the handsome Hispanic guy.

Chase started growling some scheduling information and Maggie listened with half an ear, distracted by his hands rubbing her back under her shirt. Then the conversation penetrated the lust fog in her brain and she realized he hired people. He was a building contractor. A mad idea took shape in her head.

Screw it. Desperate times called for desperate measures. If she was going to stay in Vegas, she had to make a gamble, or stick her tail between her legs and limp back to Idaho.

The talk died out. Everyone at the table was coupled up, kissing and groping each other. It was dirty: a scene that belonged in a dark house full of desperate teenagers, not the corner of a burger bar.

Maggie settled more fully against his chest, spreading her legs a little and subtly grinding down on him. He groaned, his hands gripping her hips. She could go to bed with him, easily. "Let's go," she whispered in his ear. "I'll take you to my room."

"Yes," he slurred.

He stumbled as they walked between the restaurant tables. She put an arm around his back, guiding him against her side. "Don't worry," he mumbled, his eyes squinted. "Still good for it. Been so fuckin' long."

They jolted to a stop in front of her door. She dug in her pocket for the key, startling when he pressed his front against her back, pinning her forward until she put her hands out to brace on the door.

"Get the damn door open, woman," he growled into her neck.

She blew out her breath. "You're not, um, thinking of anything super rough, are you? I'm more of a get-me-warmed-up-with-a-foot-massage kind of gal." That was a lie, although she hadn't realized it until an hour ago.

He bit her neck. She gasped, stumbling sideways as the door swung open. He grabbed her around the waist with one arm, dragging her across the floor into the little room with a big bed in the center. The door was kicked shut behind them. "I'm a beast," he muttered. He tossed her on the bed. "Take off those jeans."

"Oh." She scratched her nose. He staggered into the bathroom. Maggie glanced at the door. "Culinary school, pastry chef," she whispered. She took off her pants.

He came out pulling his shirt off over his head. She blinked, taking in stacked muscle on a wide frame, tapering down to a lean middle. He wiped his face on the bunched-up cloth then tossed it onto the floor. "Shirt too. Get a wiggle on, I'm not gonna last much longer." He pushed his jeans down, swaying on his feet.

"Come on over here and rest for a minute. Lie down and I'll—"

He pounced on her. She yelped, then grunted when he clumsily jabbed her in the chest with an elbow. Straddling her, he yanked her T-shirt up over her head, then tossed it behind his shoulder.

Humming, he put his face down on her chest, nuzzling back and forth. His beard stubble rasped over her prickling skin. She giggled, breathlessly. He bit her nipple firmly and she sucked in a breath through her teeth.

"Babe, I'm gonna have to rest for a spell before I suck on your pussy. Too dizzy, ya know?"

She shivered as he planted soft feathery kisses on her neck. "Um, what do you have in mind?"

He sat up on his knees, looking over the condoms and lube on the side table. "Roll over."

She blew out a breath. "Are you thinking keep it simple here or…"

"Fuck, my boxers are still on." He tumbled sideways, wrestling with getting the waistband down his muscular thighs.

She waited, electric tingles of anticipation curling her toes as her shallow breaths whooshed in and out of her chest. He'd wound her up, despite being a clumsy drunk. If he kept it simple, she'd get there. No way was she doing some kind of complicated anal play with him though.

"Come over here and help me with these, woman."

She pulled the boxers off him. His erection was long and thick, standing up against his abs. She sighed. Apparently, he was one of the lucky ones that could drink and still screw.

"Put a condom on me," he ordered, staring at her through slitted eyes.

She fondled him, watching his head arch back on the pillows, tendons standing out on his neck. The condom slid on tight. She stroked him with lube on her hand.

He swatted her away. Muscles bunching, he surged up off the pillows to grab her hips. She sighed, letting him turn her around and position her so her butt was up and her shoulders down, like a bitch waiting for a quick rut.

"Oh, my God, I fuckin love your ass." He stroked her butt cheeks, squeezing and pinching. His fingers found the folds between her legs. "Mm, you're wet, you naughty little pussy."

She gasped, his fingers perfectly stroking her. He spread her apart, pushing in the tip of his shaft, then leaned back to grip her hips. He lunged in hard, shoving her forward across the sheets. She braced her hands against the headboard.

His pelvis slapped her while he grunted and puffed behind her. She remembered the mirror and looked up to see him watching her. "Come on, babe," he ground out, his head falling back.

He didn't stop. She closed her eyes, the wave inside her rising higher until she shuddered. He shifted her hips, reaching around to rub her and she squirmed, gasping, shaking with release. "Yes," he moaned, slapping her behind and bucking against her. He slowed to a stop, collapsing on top of her. "I made it five minutes," he panted. "Fuck yeah."

"Lie down on the bed, beast. You weigh a ton."

He kissed her shoulders. "I should be the sex worker. All you did was lie there." He rolled sideways off her.

Maggie moved her stiff elbows gingerly. By the time she sat up, Chase was snoring. When she spread a blanket over him, he popped open one eye to glare at her, then dropped back into a deep sleep.

She crept over to his jacket and slid his wallet out of the pocket.

CHAPTER THREE

There was a tapeworm in his head playing the drums. No, that was his phone vibrating on a counter some- where. Chase rolled over and grabbed the gallon sized jug of water he kept next to his mattress. His hand knocked over an empty whiskey bottle that clattered painfully against a dish on the floor. His sheets were bunched up on the carpet and smelled foul, vomit foul.

He watched a palm tree through the uncovered window of the family room where he slept on a mattress on the floor. Living in a corner of the large house surrounded by empty beer cans and liquor bottles kept things simple. And reminded him every day what a mess he was. *I'm not a coward*, he told himself. His mantra was his counter to the nights he stumbled out into the entryway to stare up at the second-floor landing, and its drop to the marble tile below.

That girl had distracted him. His cock stirred, coming awake with hopeful twitches. Maggie. Her friend had said her name then covered her mouth and giggled. They weren't supposed to give out real names.

Maggie had disappeared. He'd passed out for about five

hours in her room last night and woken up the only one in it. Then he'd paid for a ride home.

She wasn't online with the brothel's website. She was gone. Part of him was glad. Very glad. The last thing he needed was another messed-up young woman to feel guilty about.

His work phone vibrated again. He stumbled into the kitchen and started the coffee maker then stuck his head in the sink. Cold water from the kitchen faucet beat on his cheek while he waited for the percolating to start. He found his toothbrush in a tall shot glass and the toothpaste under a pile of beer cans. Tomorrow he should go to the grocery store. He needed Bloody Mary mix.

He pulled the phone off its charger and glared at the caller ID. The pounding intensified in his head. His unhinged stalker ex-girlfriend had found another way to invade his sorry-ass life. She used his work Facebook account to flood him with messages and naked pictures. Now she had the new business cell number. He dropped the phone and pressed on his throbbing forehead with the heel of one hand.

He glared out at the morning light glimmering on the pool water in the backyard. Had he hit rock bottom yet? His mind shifted back to Afghanistan, as it did whenever he stopped moving. The flag-draped casket had been carried across the tarmac, loaded into a C-130 for shipment home. Wind and dust, his mouth dry, and the smell of diesel. And nothing good inside him anymore.

Chase squeezed the bridge of his nose. The buzzing was back in his ears. He could use more uncomplicated sex. With Maggie. Something to crack the broken video reel in his head. The phone buzzed again. He snatched it up and blocked the number. She'd start using burner cells next. He grabbed his running shoes, put on sweats and an old T-shirt from the floor, then hit the street outside.

After a few miles he was covered with sweat, a residue of alcohol on his skin. He rounded a corner and was back at his five-bedroom, two-story, balconied home. The Pool House. The other flipper he owned and the big gamble that he'd put everything into. Empty, undecorated, a shell he was squatting in until it was ready to sell.

A beat-up old brown minivan had parked in his driveway. He slowed to a walk. The van had old-school peeling-veneer wood panels on the sides and was packed to the ceiling with stuff. It looked like a homeless person lived in there.

After he passed the van parked in his driveway, he could make out a small figure wearing a large trucker ball cap sitting on the concrete floor of his front porch, slumped against the stucco wall of the house. She was in the shadow cast from the second story balcony but he recognized her. The hair raised on his arms and nape. Bending over, he rested his hands on his knees and sucked in a couple of breaths. Blonde, wearing the same jeans and T-shirt as last night.

A mangy little dog snarled at him from the window of the van then threw himself against the glass, barking. Maggie scrubbed a hand over her face and squinted up.

His brain clicked on. Heart pounding in his ears, body as tense as plywood, he marched up to her. "How the hell did you get my address?"

MAGGIE JERKED AWAKE. Leaning forward, she wiped the drool off her mouth. Toto was seriously losing his mind. She braced her forearms on her knees and looked up. "What?"

He glared at her like she'd broken his window or something. "What the fuck are you doing here? And how did you get my address?"

Maggie opened then closed her mouth, adrenaline slapping her. This wasn't how she'd imagined this going. At all. She got to her feet, none too gracefully.

"I came to see if there was any kind of work I could do for you, for your business." Maggie talked fast. "I'm a homeowner—I know about maintenance. Painting, yard work, cleaning, detail work, I can do all that and more. I've been working in restaurants since I was fourteen and it's taught me to hustle. Also I do photography, social media, customer service—"

"Stop." His nostrils flared.

Maggie swallowed and took a step back. Actually, she knew nothing about this man, and the tendons bulging out in his neck and jaw spoke to her of serious anger-management issues.

"Answer my question," he barked. "How do you know where I live? I work hard to keep that private."

Maggie tripped a little as she edged sideways. She was dizzy, her stomach empty and twirling. "Well, I, um, took a photo of your driver's license after you passed out. Also, I borrowed the forty in cash I found in your wallet."

"Right," he said through his teeth, "you can tell a cop all about it after I file a police report."

She put up her hands. "I just wanted to ask you for a job. Look, you can search my phone—I'll erase the photo and you'll never see me again. I don't have a copy of your address written down anywhere. I'll delete it out of my crappy phone right now."

"Fine." He brushed past her and went into the house, slamming the door behind him.

Maggie moved quickly off the front porch to her van. A wave of dizziness hit her and she leaned against the warm surface, letting her hat fall to the ground. Her chest was tight. She massaged across her sternum, trying to get air moving through her constricted throat. *Damn it*. She was such an idiot.

Toto whined inside the van, reaching a paw out through the cracked window. What did she think the man was going to do when he found out she'd gotten into his wallet, stolen his address and taken his cash? Thank her for stopping by?

A hand grasped her elbow. Toto rammed the window. Maggie jumped, knocking her head against the rearview mirror. She yanked away from the grasp and spun around.

It was Chase, glaring at her, one hand still up in the air. "Get in the house."

"No, thank you, but no." Maggie backed away from him. "I'm, um, not feeling very well and better get going."

He sighed and looked up at the sky. "I'm willing to talk about employment."

Maggie swallowed. If Toto kept up the ferocious intensity, his heart might burst. She used her T-shirt sleeve to blot the sweat on her face. Dealing with an unhinged man was way too much excitement for eight a.m. But she was desperate. "Okay, let's talk right here."

Chase closed his eyes and took a deep breath. "I lost my temper, but it's fine now. I would never hurt a woman."

"Uh-huh." Maggie bent over to pick up her hat. The man was giving her whiplash. As she stood up, her dangling keys were snatched out of her hands.

"Hey." She pulled her hat on to get the sun out of her eyes. Chase was already marching through his front door.

She pushed off the van and followed him through the glass paned heavy wooden doors, and stopped. The entryway was a vast, two-story space with a very pretty chandelier hanging from the ceiling. A wide staircase bent up to the second floor, the honeyed oak railing continuing onto the interior balconies on the second story. The house was massive, with white pedestaled columns under the archways on the main floor. It would be a good place to enact a modern version of Romeo and Juliet, one that took place in the nineties, with high-tops and neon jackets.

Chase cleared his throat. He was leaning against a wall to the side of the open front door.

Maggie stayed in the doorway. "You have my keys," she said. "And I'm not comfortable being in here alone with you. You've gone from murderous rage to thief in the last three minutes."

"Turnabout is fair play. And murder is not what I have in mind for you. Not relaxing enough."

She crossed her arms. "This was a bad idea," she said. "I've got poor impulse control. I'm sorry about your license." She held out her hand. "Just toss me those keys and I'll get out of your hair."

They stared at each other. She managed to keep a bland expression on her face but knew a flush was creeping across her cheeks. Slowly, he put her keys in his pocket. Then he crooked a finger at her.

"I'll wait in my van until you change your mind," she said, taking a step back.

"Maggie—"

"Wait, how do you know my name?"

"Your friend let it slip last night. I saw her when I was searching for you."

Maggie frowned and waited for him to continue.

"Are you livin' in that minivan?"

She stared up at the wide curving staircase. "Temporarily."

"That's not safe."

"Yeah, somebody might steal my keys and corner me in a creepy house."

"This house isn't creepy."

"Right, the liquor bottles on the bottom steps of the stairs add a homey touch."

He squinted at her. "I'm sorry I lost my temper. I have someone harassing me right now so I'm careful to keep my address private."

She scratched her nose. She knew his type and had made it a policy to steer clear. He was a drunk, short tempered and high strung, likely to be violently jealous and controlling, and too self-involved to care for anyone. Also, probably an extremely exciting lover when he wasn't drunk, her brain threw in unhelpfully. She squeezed her thighs together.

"Come over here and I'll give you your keys."

With a fatalistic sigh, she edged toward him, watching his face. He was in resting tiger mode—just a big pretty cat, luring in stupid little birds and butterflies who liked his stripes. She stopped in front of him and held her hand out. "Keys and a french fry, please."

He pounced, grabbing her hand and pulling her against him. Knocking off her hat, he smashed his parted lips against hers, his tongue pushing into her mouth. She jerked, shocked but unresisting. Or maybe it was that he affected her, the slutty sex addict she kept chained inside herself, and that she'd been thinking about him all night. The sex hadn't been much—but there was something about him. His hands rubbed along her body, pushing her arms up and placing her hands behind his neck. She turned her head, heaving in a breath.

"Stop." She pushed at him. It was moving too fast—his erection was hard enough to drive nails. His hands were cupping her bottom and pulling her up against him. "I can't do this, Chase, please stop."

He groaned and let go of her, turning himself against the wall. A phone alarm blared to life, going off somewhere in the house.

"Shit," he said, "I've got to get to a job." He took off through an opening by the stairs toward what looked like the kitchen and family room area. A second later, the alarm stopped. He darted into another room and she heard a shower start.

She slid down the wall and sat down. Her lips were bruised. She'd never been kissed like that in her life.

Ten minutes later, Chase emerged, hair wet and socks in his hands. "Stay here." He bent over next to a pair of work boots tucked in a corner. "Do whatever. I'll pay you."

Maggie stood up. "Where are my keys?"

He paused, looking back at the bathroom. She tensed, wondering if he would try to take them with him. "They're in my sweatpants pocket," he said. "Stay here. There's cash on the kitchen counter. I'll be back in five hours."

CHAPTER FOUR

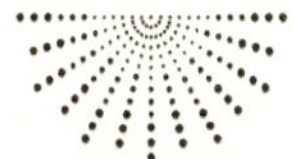

Maggie ran toward her keys. What sounded like a garage door opened and an engine revved outside. Inside the bathroom, it was moist, woodsy soap lingering in the air. The sweatpants were crumpled in a corner of the white tiled bathroom, along with his sweat-soaked T-shirt. She crouched down and felt a hard metal shape, exhaling in relief. Standing up, she slipped the keys firmly in her pocket.

"Keep calm and eat cupcakes," she whispered. Was he really gone?

Her heart beat fast in her chest as she crossed her arms and chewed on her bottom lip. She walked back to the foyer and peeped out the front door, standing still and listening. Chase was gone—he'd said for five hours. She should leave.

Instead, she got Toto out of the van and brought him inside on his leash. They walked down the hallway, Toto with his nose on the ground, and she had her first view of the kitchen. The counters were obscured by piles of beer cans, stacked into pyramids and tall towers, and lined up liquor bottles. The space was large, a U-shaped layout, with a kitchen nook attached, and divided from the spacious family room by a long bar.

Through the wall of windows she could see a stunning backyard with a large winding pool surrounded by intricate landscaping. Not able to stop herself, she walked into the family room. There was a fireplace on one wall and a bare mattress on the floor. His bed, apparently. Clothes were piled around the room, most of them dirty on the carpet. She coughed, her nose wrinkled up. The place was stale and dusty with trash on every surface.

For some insane reason the man trusted her alone in his large house—after looking like his head was going to explode with rage, and then threatening to call the police. In the kitchen he'd left three hundred dollars on the counter, tucked under a bottle of Jack Daniels. She massaged her temples as her phone rang. Andy. Again. She was texting him once a day but he wanted to talk. *Nope.* She silenced the call and put her phone back.

There were also several calls and messages from old Mr. Filch, her lawyer. If he didn't see some money that week, he'd said, she'd force him to take action.

She slumped into the old camp chair beside a beat-up folding table, the only furniture besides the mattress on the floor. Toto limped over and jumped up onto her lap and licked her face.

"Toto, we're not in Idaho anymore."

Chase was some kind of vampire man who felt the need to enthrall her into becoming his sex servant. A perverse part of her wanted to walk into his arms and forget about everything. Let him pay her for sex. The excitement with him could last a day, a week, maybe a bit longer, and then she'd be alone again.

She cleaned out a mug and poured herself a cup of coffee. *What choice do I have?* She'd left Idaho a week ago and already her unpaid bills, not to mention Mr. Filch, were about to bury her and repossess her trailer. Today, she'd work on the mess and be gone long before Chase got back.

Eight hours later, Maggie pulled into the Red Rock Canyon Campground, a parking lot in the middle of the desert. Jagged mountain peaks surrounded the little valley. The sky was a brilliant blue over the rich red, brown, and deep yellow landscape. At the visitor board it explained that the striated layers of the mountain's cliffs, rising out of the ground like buildings right in front of her, were multicolored sandstone and limestone.

The cliff walls looked a bit like puff pastry folded around layers of citrus and baked blueberry. Maggie fed Toto then pulled out the burrito she'd brought with her and sat on her campsite's picnic table to eat.

After not really sleeping the night before, she would lie down in her van as soon as it got dark, in an hour. There were signs of other campers about, and a handful of people cooking over propane stoves close by. She liked the sound of their easy conversation and low chuckling. With Red Rock Canyon next door, this campground saw a lot of rock climbers, hikers, and other outdoor nature nerds wealthy enough to buy the gear and have the time. Maybe she'd join them one day.

Her phone buzzed. "Hey, Princess, how's the sex trade?"

"Oh, my gawd, Maggie," mumbled Princess, her words barely understandable. "Where the fuck are you?"

"You don't have someone's dingle in your mouth right now, do you?"

"Shut up," she said clearly. "Gawd, you're disgusting. I'm putting on lipstick, okay, because I'm about to make another shit ton of money. So, I'll repeat myself, where the fuck are you?"

"I'm camping." Maggie pulled out the cheap air mattress

she'd bought earlier that day. "Red Rock Canyon. It's gorgeous, and a little dusty." A gust of wind swirled reddish dirt around her feet.

"I can't believe you left like that last night without even talking to me. That guy you were with paid for a full package and you didn't even take your money. What's wrong with you? What are you doing?"

"Are you yelling at me because I didn't stay to be your brothel buddy?"

"Well, duh. After I got you this job and everything."

"I chickened out. It's a shame, considering how hard up I am for cash."

"No shit, honey. I don't think they'd take you back now that this other girl has your spot and she's, like, ready for anything. I mean anything. She's loud and tacky and I'm sick of her." Princess paused, spraying something. "I can't believe that hot piece of delicious that was all over you last night."

"He has rage issues." Maggie paused, not sure she wanted to ask the next question. Her mouth opened anyway. "When's your day off? Do you want to come into the city and get some coffee with me?"

"Drive sixty miles for coffee? Fuck that. But yeah, let's do a girls' day. I need some time away from these catty bitches."

"I'll still be broke so I'll tag along while you do whatever."

"Relax. If you take care of me, I might even treat you to some fun."

Maggie wrinkled her nose up and held the phone away from her face to look at it. What the heck did that mean?

"Shit," Princess said, "there's the bell. Later, poor Maggie."

While Maggie stretched out in the back of her minivan, warm enough in her sleeping bag with Toto curled up next to her, she flipped through a cookbook and tried not to think about Chase. Tomorrow would be Sunday—he'd probably take the day off. Her stomach flipped and chills danced down her spine. Last night she'd been considering something with him, wrestling with it, eventually planning to ask for a real job and also date him—as in, he asks her out and she says yes, with no money exchanged.

Her body reacted again to what had happened that morning—shoulders tightening but also a coil of heat at her core. She would not sign up for that kind of torture. The important thing was she had said no and he had stopped. She would be firm and set up some boundaries. She sighed. Why did such an attractive man have to be so twisted?

Her phone pinged with another text from Andy. *I'm coming to find you*, was written along with a dozen questions asking where she was. She turned off her screen.

CHASE SAT at his clean kitchen island drinking coffee. The cold leftover pizza slice he had swallowed roiled around in his hungover gut. He looked down at the note she'd left yesterday. He'd memorized the damn thing.

> *Chase, I'll be back tomorrow morning with groceries. And to talk about a job. I won't sleep with you and that's final. Try not to fall in the pool again, Maggie.*

The layers of boozy filth he'd created around his hovel hole in the house had been transformed into a tidy clear space. He had spent weeks stacking those beer cans and felt a little mournful to see them gone. And relieved. His bed had clean sheets and a blanket on it. The toilet didn't look like a nightmare from a gas station and the floor was clear of broken glass and take-out garbage. It even got him thinking about buying a vacuum easier to use than a shop-vac.

His phone rang again. He let it go to voice mail. It was his cousin, Lucas, wanting to know where he lived so that he could come over and "hang out." In fraternity speak that meant create a mini golf tournament in your backyard and break a window. And that was just the last time Lucas had shown up with "a few friends."

Since Chase had moved into The Pool House a couple of months ago, he'd held out against Lucas and his aunt, who both lived in the area. The isolation had allowed for great things to happen, like his beer-can pyramid. Family tended to get in the way when you were headed toward rock bottom. Also, if Lucas saw the pool in the backyard, he'd try to relocate the fraternity.

> I'm working all the time. Fuck off.

LUCAS

It's worse than I thought. You need an intervention.

> I'll intervention your face. Go study Lucas. You're there to learn not find new swimming pools to get drunk in.

I knew you had a swimming pool you fuck!

> I didn't say that. You're as transparent as a blood sucking mosquito.

I'm your cousin and I'm concerned about you. Concerned that you're becoming a shit-eating hermit.

> I'll leave that to you and the pile of vomit you sleep in at night.

Yeah, he was a miserable hypocrite.

He closed his phone and set it, screen down, on the counter. Why the hell hadn't he gotten her cell phone number? Yesterday he'd managed to get home an hour early and started cursing as soon as he saw the empty driveway. After his flare of rage had passed, he'd fretted all night like the mother of a virgin on prom night. Gone. He didn't even know her last name.

He went back out to the front porch, where he'd been waiting for the last hour. It was still early. She'd taken the cash and promised to buy groceries. So far, she did what she said she would. And she'd decided she wasn't sleeping with him. Chase rubbed his face, pacing back and forth.

A brown, mud-splattered minivan turned onto his street, the engine clanking. There was Maggie, leaning forward as she drove, little dog in her lap, sunglasses perched on her face. He sagged against the stucco wall, his mouth dry. *Get a grip, Chase.*

She shut down the spluttering engine and jumped out of the driver-side door. Walking briskly to the passenger side, she opened it to reveal the seat covered with grocery bags. Grabbing two plastic bags in each hand, she pivoted so quickly the eight pack of paper towels under her chin flew out onto the driveway.

"Stocking up for a siege?" he asked, and she jumped. The little terrier dog ran forward, putting his tiny body in front of her, and growled at him. He bent over to pick up the towels. "What is all this?"

"Holy hickory, you startled me." She took a step back, keeping the grocery bags between them. "This is food and cleaning supplies. Chase, meet groceries. Groceries, meet Chase. The inside of your fridge was the most depressing sight I've ever seen. I had to do something."

He grabbed the rest of the bags, ignoring the dog, not sure what he wanted to say to her. She was beautiful, even rumpled with her hair pulled back in a low ponytail and her face sweaty. He should try to explain the tangled knot of emotion that sometimes overwhelmed him. Mostly he needed to go back in time to when they still touched each other and he could kiss her until she wrapped her legs around his waist…He swallowed.

She whistled and the dog trotted after her into the house, looking over his shoulder to growl at Chase. He followed them into the kitchen, liking the way Maggie's hips twitched from side to side.

"Where'd you go last night?"

She started pulling things out of the bags. "Well, first I went to the Centennial Hills Library to get online and do some research. I found a campground I liked, it had space, so I shopped then headed out there." She bent over, putting things in the cabinet under the sink. He caught his breath—that ass was too good. He noticed a bulge in her back pocket. "It was nice. Clean bathrooms and people doing yoga in the morning."

He closed his eyes, blocking out her tight blue T-shirt for a moment. She was like predator bait on a stick. "Text me your phone number," he said tersely.

She paused, her eyebrows raised. "Give me your number on some paper," she said carefully. His right eye started twitching. "I want to see how today goes before we exchange cell phone info."

Heat exploded in his body. "I'm not fucking capable of not sleeping with you so *please* just fucking get used to the idea," he ground out, not shouting. By much.

"Chase," she said, taking a step away. Toto sprang forward and nipped at his leg. It hurt and he barely resisted kicking the damn thing. "No, Toto." She picked the dog up. "I can't do this with you. You're 'not a relationship guy' and that's pretty clear by the way you're living."

He shoved his hands in his pockets. "Looks nice in here now."

"I grew up with alcoholics," she continued, "and it's not something I can deal with in my partner. Real and meaningful—that's what I want. Not just sex."

"It wouldn't be 'just' sex with me, babe. It will be fucking until you find enlightenment."

"I'm telling you no," she said. "If you can't respect that, then I need to go."

He pounced forward, pulling her against his front. She squealed and struggled, the dog snarling and twisting in her arms. He pulled the cell phone out of her back pocket then let her go.

"I'm getting your cell number," he said, pretending to be reasonable. "The rest of it we'll figure out later."

She huffed, the look on her face promising bad things as he used her phone to text himself. The dog finally stopped barking, subdued to low growls by whatever treat she was feeding him. She put him back on the ground where he stood, glaring at Chase, next to her feet.

He blew out a breath. "I'm not going to give this back, yet," he said, waving her phone at her, "because I don't want you to leave, and it's my turn to talk." She leaned against the counter and crossed her arms. He walked over to the chair and sat down. "Yeah, I'm fucked up and not life-partner material. But that doesn't mean I don't have anything to offer you."

"You want to pay me for sex," she said in a flat voice.

"Yes. And to do all this housewarming stuff too if it makes you feel better. Let's figure this out—come to some kind of understanding. You could stay here for one, it's a hell of a lot safer than camping."

"Not with you around." Hard turquoise eyes stared back at him.

"Fine. We won't sleep together today," he said.

She snorted, her face pinched.

"But keep that little black apron ready because I'm going to see you in it soon." He placed her phone on the counter.

She opened the pack of paper towels with a violent rip. "I'll work today then," she said, her tone cold. "But I'll burn that apron before I wear it for you again."

CHAPTER FIVE

Maggie put her earbuds in, hands shaking, with her back to Chase. She hit play without caring what it was. A fast and sad bluegrass song blasted into her head. She grabbed the bottle of Simple Green and turned to the fridge. Tomorrow she would find a restaurant job, even if it was cleaning bathrooms for the yellow arches. *Culinary school, pastry chef...*

Chase sat at the beat-up folding table in the breakfast nook, typing on a laptop. A cold piece of sandwich bread from the loaf she'd bought that morning was beside him. She sighed, jiggling her jaw to relax her clenched face. He seemed like the kind of guy who could fix anything and yet he was constitutionally incapable of caring for himself.

She should let him stew in his alcohol fumes—but she'd already bought all the food. Plus, she was starving.

While sausage fried, she grated cheese and opened salsa and sour cream containers. She put out bananas and apples in a bowl on the counter, reluctantly pleased when Chase started eating fruit. It was her curse, the need to feed people.

In another pan she scrambled a big batch of eggs with butter and warmed up tortillas in the microwave.

She dumped a plate down on the table next to Chase without looking at him. He kept typing. Her ancient MP3 player switched over to disco music and she bustled around the kitchen, cleaning up and eating her own breakfast. In the fridge she left four more breakfast burritos, prepped to go in the microwave with heating instructions written on top.

When she looked up, Chase was staring at her, almost smiling. She flushed and turned away.

She was sliding a tray of chocolate chip cookies with walnuts into the oven when someone punched the front door three times. Toto growled and shot out of the room to bark in the entryway.

Whoever it was pressed on the doorbell, making it ding-dong ding-dong without stopping. Maggie yanked her earbuds out. Chase was at the table with his head in his hands.

"Should I get the hot tar ready?" she shouted over the doorbell and Toto barking. "We could dump it from the upstairs balcony."

"Let's pretend like we're not here," he shouted back.

"Nope." She grabbed a long spatula and a rolling pin. "I'm gonna shove that doorbell down their throat." Armed and ready, she ignored whatever he yelled at her and stomped to the front door. Chase grabbed her elbow as she swung open the door. Toto sprang out to growl and lunge at the invader.

A young man was on the porch, leaning against the door jamb, eating a potato chip. His hand froze when he saw her. Then a slow grin broke out over his face.

"Shove off, Lucas," said Chase in a cold voice. "I'm busy today."

"Not a chance, cuz. Let me in or I'm calling my mom." Lucas winked at Maggie.

"He has a mother?" Maggie said to Chase. She patted her leg and Toto ran back inside.

Lucas ducked in past her, sidling sideways when Toto growled. He finger-combed his brown hair, styled in a slight wave on top and cropped short on the sides. Thin sideburns, carefully trimmed, angled down his smooth boyish face. He was big like his cousin but softer with thin forearms and a bit of pudge around his middle. He stared at her, an easy grin on his face.

Chase glanced out the door at the car idling in his driveway. "Who the hell are those assholes?"

"My compatriots and technology savants. They used GPS technology to track your phone. Fucking radomatic. What the shit are you doing, cuz?" Lucas looked around the foyer, bag of potato chips dangling from one hand. "This is pimp. It's like nineties glamorous—fucking perfect for a dance party. Shit man, I'm like ten minutes away."

"Lucas," Chase said in a hard voice that startled her, "you've got no claim or right to this house. It's an investment and if you so much as scuff the floor, I'm going to wipe it off with your face. I'm fucking serious."

"Relax." Lucas absently glanced down the hallway to the left of the stairs. "Are there cookies baking?" He wandered off toward the kitchen. Maggie stared at Chase, her mouth hanging open. He pressed his fingers into the bridge of his nose and groaned. She chuckled and followed his cousin.

She found him frozen in place, staring out at the backyard.

"Holy donkfunkulous," he gasped, putting a hand on the glass and leaning forward. Maggie grinned. The backyard was ridiculous, something a Disney resort would envy. A donut-shaped pool meandered through palm trees with wooden bridges crossing over the turquoise water. The center island was decked out as a tiki bar, complete with lagoon barstools, Polynesian art, and a barbecue. There was a hot tub and water slide built into the natural stone design. Lucas took a deep breath, hand over his heart, and turned to her.

"Oh yeah, and who are you, snazcat?"

CHASE'S SANCTUARY was thoroughly invaded. He wanted to punch something but knew from experience how tedious a dented wall was to fix. He settled for pulling at his hair with both hands.

In the kitchen, Maggie leaned across the kitchen island and smiled at Lucas while he ate one of her cookies. His cookies. He clenched his teeth.

"Yeah," said Maggie. The red haze in Chase's brain cleared enough for him to tune in. "I need to establish residency for a year before I can enroll at CSN in-state."

"College of Southern Nevada—huge campus. What will you study?"

"Culinary arts, focused on pastry. Until then, I'm working as a personal chef and other odd jobs until I can get into a professional kitchen."

"Radalicious."

Chase froze, a little gut shot. They hadn't gotten around to talking about what Maggie was doing with her life. Hearing it now made him feel like an asshole. *Hell.* Back up, yeah, she'd made him obsessed with sex but fucking look at her. Lucas kept lobbing more questions.

"I'm from Idaho," Maggie said. "My granny, who raised me, died from blood cancer about a year ago. I stayed with her after high school to help out. Once I'd paid off the funeral expenses, I decided it was time to move over here and get going with my career."

Chase's stomach dropped. His uncomplicated lust for her twisted into something too unwieldy to manage.

Lucas cleared his throat. "Shit—condolences…"

"Thanks. What about you?"

"I'm at UNLV studying communication and marketing." Lucas took another cookie. "So, you're like Chase's cook?"

"Lucas," he barked, "back off with the twenty questions. Hustle your ass over to your fraternity house before you miss a meal."

"It's Winter Break. Besides, we're on our own on Sundays. Most people eat off campus, like with their families."

"You're not my family, you're a plague. I need to work."

"Cuz, it's clear to me you've turned yourself into a socially inept loner. If you have any guns, turn them over now for the good of society." Chase took a step toward him. "Besides," said Lucas holding out a hand, "my mom's upset with you for not telling her where you live."

Chase paused. "Fine," he ground out, "you can stay for another cookie. Then you're gone."

"I bought five pounds of chicken to barbecue," said Maggie, shooting Chase a grin. "There's plenty to share. Lucas, can you get that grill going for me out back?"

"In a rad-ass minute I can," he said, a smarmy smile on his cheesy face.

And just like that, Chase was out-maneuvered in his own house. He retreated to his computer, grumbling, but the two young idiots ignored him. Five minutes later, he glared out the back window and there were more man-boys and a tall skinny brunette standing with Lucas and Maggie, laughing and drinking beer. Someone started playing pop music out of a smartphone. He was totally, stupidly, invaded.

Maggie came back in and bustled around the kitchen, Toto trotting beside her feet, her big sunglasses reflecting sunbeams of light. He stood up and propped himself against a counter, watching her. She stacked wrapped sandwiches in his fridge. Marinating chicken filled a big metal bowl. She must have brought in the cooking tools she was using. He owned a collection of plastic take-out utensils and a few coffee mugs. There was tomato, parsley, and cucumber on a bamboo cutting board. Chopped fresh garlic sizzling in butter sat on the stove in a stainless-steel pan.

She paused to look at him, an eyebrow raised. He wanted to kiss her. He put his hands in his pockets and cleared his throat. "You know I'm not going to force you to sleep with me," he said.

"Do I?"

"A thousand dollars a week."

She froze, her eyes wide.

"That's a salary that includes cooking, cleaning, and detail work on my renovations. Things like sanding drywall and painting." She blinked at him, a hand over her heart. "You'll have a credit card for expenses: food, supplies I need and so on. Oh, and I'll need personal-assistant help more than anything—calling clients, returning emails, plaguing me with scheduling issues."

She was quiet, staring at him while her fingers twitched. He scrubbed a hand over his face. The girl was too inappropriately attractive.

"It's a generous offer," she finally said. "But I'm not sure… you're pretty intense about getting into my pants. And controlling my freedom to transport and communication. I'm not sure it's a good idea for either of us."

"Honey," he said, "this—the clean house, food, folded laundry and so on—has tamed me already. I'll enter into a lease agreement with you so that you can start getting your residency." She perked up, leaning forward. "And, you can stay here until you find your own place."

She shook her head. "I'm not sleeping here," she said. "Can we do the lease on one of your other properties?"

"No." He leaned back against the counter. "I'll sublet that room off the entryway to you, with the French doors."

Maggie dumped rice into the pan with garlic. "I'll try working for you for a week," she said. "But I'm getting my own place."

CHAPTER SIX

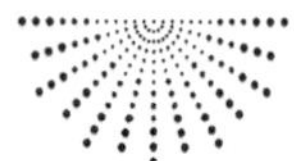

Maggie shivered. The wind howled hard enough to shake her van. She scooted down further into her sleeping bag. Coyotes yipped, snarled, barked, and mournfully sang in the hills close by. Toto was standing up on his hind feet with his nose pressed against the rear window.

Of course, now she had to pee. Walking outside to use the campsite bathroom in the middle of the night meant watching for snakes, their dark spear-headed shapes moving at terrifying speeds in the beam of her flashlight. After that experience, if she woke up and had a full bladder she held it.

The sky cracked with a rip of thunder. Her eyes flew open. Golf-ball-sized pellets of rain battered down on the roof of the minivan. Toto climbed back down to his bed and curled up beside her air mattress.

Sighing, she flipped open her cell phone. Dim blue light from the screen illuminated her water bottle and pile of cookbooks. Why did rain make you need to pee more?

Before she could stop herself, she was reading the texts from Chase again. The last few days she'd hardly seen him, getting there when he was on his way out the door and leaving before he got home. That was what she wanted—had to have. A minute in the same room as him and she was a little hot under the collar. Okay, if she was being honest with herself, the heat went everywhere.

He had called her several times a day with things he needed, like pricing on luxury toilets. One of his clients wanted a toilet that cost $8,599.50. What do you get for all that money? A toilet seat that knows when you're approaching, raises its lid, turns on some toilet music, and warms up the seat. Creepy.

Earlier that night, he had texted her trying to get her to come back and go out to dinner with him on the strip in Vegas. She'd said no. She read again what he'd written after that.

CHASE

Let me know if you need ANYTHING. Don't get into trouble because you're being stubborn.

When she hadn't responded he'd texted again.

You okay out there? Any creepy guys in vans? Need someone to warm you up?

She'd written back that she was fine. She didn't mention being cold.

CHASE

Goodnight.

And then a minute later:

Tell me goodnight.

She'd written back goodnight.

CHASE

Okay goodnight. XX

It was the beer making him cheesy. Even so, it gave her the warm fuzzies, a bit. She shook her head at herself and pressed a hand on her forehead. A little careless affection and she darted for it like a starving dog after a crust of bread.

In the mornings he was hungover and surly. She kept her distance, and he didn't have much time. Except he always managed to get in a few terse questions about how camping was going, like had anyone bothered her, and did all the locks work on her van. And he'd started making friends with Toto, mostly by tossing a hunk of meat or cheese on the floor when he thought she wasn't looking.

Yesterday, she'd filled up his canteen with coffee, warmed up his breakfast to go, and packed his lunch before he was out of the shower. While he was in the room with her, he'd mumbled and grumbled about things that needed to get done. She'd still been able to hear his truck in the driveway when she'd gotten a text from him saying, *You're amazing. Thank you, Maggie.*

The first day she'd let in a crew of guys to haul out all the carpet in the house. With a start she'd realized they were the guys from the brothel. They'd done a few double takes too. But the crew had been polite and worked quick, thankfully. Most of her was desperately glad that her association with Chase was temporary because soon she'd be unconnected with anyone that knew she'd spent a night working in a brothel.

Still, she found herself counting down the time until she'd see him again and get another dose of body zings. They did have chemistry—the kind you don't know really exists until you find it. She covered her face with her sleeping bag and forced herself to close her eyes. *I'm a sensible person. I will choose a nice man.*

She finally dozed off in the wee hours of the morning. After sleeping through her alarm, she dragged herself in later than usual. Chase was gone, the bathroom redolent of his tangy soap. She texted him to let him know she was there.

CHASE

All right. There may be punishment for your tardy attendance.

We don't have that kind of relationship BOSS. Keep your mind out of the gutter.

Her phone pinged seconds later.

CHASE

I'll show you the gutter. And you'll like it.

She stared up at the ceiling, ashamed of the flare of desire in her nether regions. He was impossible. She had to get another job.

She made herself a cup of coffee and cleaned up Chase's dishes and beer cans. He was drinking less, she thought—he hadn't touched hard liquor all week. Yesterday she'd noticed the warm sun-kissed tone of his skin, ruddy across his nose where his hat didn't shade. He kept his beard long enough not to be bristly but still showing his angled chin and strong jaw.

Firmly she placed her coffee mug down on the table that held his computer, shuddering out a sigh of frustration with herself. *Stop thinking about that dang face*—dark eyes, with darker eyebrows arched imperiously over them. *La la la...*

They had worked out a system for her to take care of his emails. She clicked through his inbox, sorting out and erasing the junk. He'd said he didn't want to know about personal emails unless someone was dying. The implication being that she should read all of them—which she did because she couldn't resist. He didn't get many but hadn't been reading them for a long time. He had a couple of brothers and parents who all wanted him home for Christmas—they promised to call him. She shuffled another one from his aunt into the personal folder and scanned the contents. His aunt wanted to know if he was okay and wondered why he hadn't responded to her. Maggie sighed. She'd try to get Chase to dictate a response soon.

She summarized his work emails into one long message and updated his calendar with confirmations of appointments and jobs. She returned polite responses to any inquiries into working with him, letting them know he had received their email and what was next in the process. There was a ton of it every day. It boggled her mind how he'd been keeping up with everything.

One of the requests for a work bid turned out to be a Trojan horse with an ex-girlfriend inside. *Chase, you're not good for anyone but me. I'm the only one that knows what you need. That wants it. Badly. I want anything you'll give me. Put your hard punishing hands...*It went on in more graphic detail about how ready she was. What she was doing to herself as she wrote it. What she was wearing.

Maggie blinked. She had pushed herself away from the table. Her cheeks were burning hot. She wanted to squirt vinegar in this girl's eyes. Burning charcoals ignited in her chest. Holy hickory, she was jealous.

Were those BDSM references? That kind of made sense when she thought about it. He was a twisty control freak and he wanted to pay her to sleep with him. The implication was that he would be totally in charge. She swallowed.

Why was the ex-girlfriend contacting him through a work email widget? She leaned forward, tapping gently on the table. In his settings, he'd recently blocked several email addresses from contacting him. Before she could examine what she was doing too closely, she erased the dirty message from his email. And emptied the digital trash.

CHASE JUMPED out of his truck and grabbed the large box in the bed of the pickup. It was a fancy German-made vacuum he'd bought for her—for the house—today. Christmas was a couple of days away and there was only one thing he wanted. He managed to stop himself from running up to the front door.

She was there, the intensely ugly minivan parked in his driveway. The damn work phone vibrated in his back pocket. He only had about thirty minutes before the crew would be looking around like lost chicks for their heat lamp.

Inside the house a pumpkin pie had been baking and something chocolate, not a bad combination. On his way to the kitchen, he realized she was in the bathroom. Taking a shower. Humming to herself. He stared at the doorknob while his cock shook. A step back brought him against a wall. He crossed his arms and waited.

The door opened and a rosy-cheeked, towel-turbaned Maggie emerged. Unfortunately, she was wearing clothes, a fuzzy pink sweaterdress type of thing that dropped to her knees. Her legs and feet were bare, he noted with appreciation. That dress hugged her curves damned efficiently. She gasped and took a step away.

"What are you doing here?"

"I'm Chase," he said. "I live here." She smelled all soapy and hot, her smooth skin pink and clean. He was a kettle on the boil, steam whistling out of his ears.

She bit her bottom lip. He groaned. "Do you want me to make you a sandwich?" she said.

It was too much. The word want unleashed him, broke whatever freaky control had kept him in check for the last week. He stepped forward and pinned her against the door-jamb with his body. She squeaked, her hands coming up to his chest.

"I want you," he said, pushing his hips forward, "to be here when I get home." He leaned over and bit her earlobe. She gasped, her body jerking. "I'm going to kiss you now, Maggie."

Her mouth was ready and waiting for him. Their lips clung together, tongues tasting and stroking. His hands slid up and down her sides, the fuzzy fabric of the dress bunching in his fists, the hem creeping up higher. He was feverish. So ready his cock burned. *Not now,* he kept telling himself, *not enough time—it'll scare her off*...But his body was in a state of rebellion.

He grabbed her ass and hoisted her up onto his hips, her back against a wall, his groin finally finding her center. He thrust against her through his jeans, pleasure arching through him. Her underwear felt warm and wet when his fingers grazed the soft strip between her legs. She moaned, her hips bucking against him. He was lost, his mouth on her neck, ready to unzip his fly, tear off the thin cotton under his fingers.

"Chase!" She pushed against him.

"No, babe, please..."

"Chase, put me down." She struggled. *Damn it*. He let her slide down his body, holding her tight against him for an extra second.

"Let go of me."

He did. His hands were balled up, his whole body tense.

He wanted her. And hated her. How could she tease him like this?

Her eyes were huge, and her wet curly hair hung on either side of her face, the towel on the floor by her feet. He turned around and left without another word.

CHAPTER SEVEN

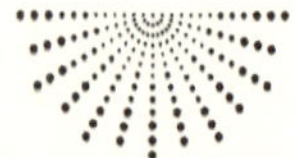

Two days later, on Christmas day, Maggie's van took its sweet time starting. Driving into town for a hot meal had been a bad idea. Wind shook her door and rattled the side view mirror. She patted the steering wheel, cooing endearments, promising an oil change soon. The van groaned, spluttered, then shook to life. She leaned back in her rumbling seat and closed her eyes. She had a bad feeling.

Going to Chase's house flashed through her mind. She'd avoided him since the kiss, leaving his house well before he was done working, and there had been no flirty text messages at night. He was less than a mile away. Except, he would take it as an invitation and she wasn't ready. Wait, no. Sex was not an option. *Ever*.

Palm trees bent sideways as wind gusts punched down the highway. She swallowed, gripping the steering wheel tightly with both hands. The storm was ratcheting up. The local weather woman had said they were in for an intense rain shower with flooding likely. Thirty agonizing minutes later, she pulled into a deserted campground, choosing the spot closest to the bathroom.

She lay her head down on the wheel and gasped as the van rocked in a gust of wind. *This is what it sounds like to be in a popcorn machine.* Rain lashed at the windows. Water puddled in deep mini ponds all over the ground.

She forced herself to move to the back of the van, setting up her bed, laying out her lights and books. Then she threw on her jacket, put on Toto's leash, and stepped out into the storm to use the toilet.

The air was fresh and pungent with camphor, citrus, and wood. In their display cabinet, the librarians had set up information about the creosote bush, which released a resinous scent when it rained. Maggie breathed it in. She could sit out on one of the covered picnic tables and watch the desert in the rain until sunset.

She squinted at the site divisions on her way back to the van. *Dang it.* She'd parked across two spaces. Not that it would matter with the campground mostly empty, but it was the kind of thing the old ranger would feel compelled to comment on. She'd brought him cookies a couple of times and now he considered himself entitled to treat her like an idiot teenager—in a curmudgeony but caring way. She jumped back in the van and turned the key.

Nothing happened. The lights didn't come on, the engine didn't turn over. *No.* She kept trying. *No, no, no.* She popped the hood and got out to stare at the dirty engine. Gingerly, she wiggled the battery connectors. They were hot and corroded. She wiped her fingers on her jeans and tried the ignition again. Nothing.

The rain was coming down in buckets. Desperately, she walked around the campground with Toto looking for other people. The ranger wasn't there. There were a couple of other cars. She knocked softly on the window of a little Camry sedan, holding her breath. No one emerged from behind the sunshades covering the windows. She ran across the muddy ground to a parked SUV. Both cars were empty.

She sat down, shivering, on one of the covered picnic tables and stared at her dark van, puddles growing around all four tires. Toto limped over and crawled onto her lap, burrowing against her as he tried to get warm. She sniffed, blotting her nose. *Shizzle, shoot, and sham.*

Possibly her worst Christmas ever. She took a drink of the single beer she'd brought out with her. The wind howled and she laughed, wiping her wet face on her shirt.

CHASE TOOK A SIP OF WHISKEY, relishing the burn on his fiery throat. He watched the rain lashing his back window. She was out there driving around in that piece-of-shit death trap on wheels. Hell of a way to spend Christmas. Not his problem. He'd pay her for a couple more weeks then shoo her off to find her own way in the city of commercial kitchens. It was for the best. He needed to concentrate on what mattered: not living a good life and searching out meaningless sex.

He had a fridge full of food and he didn't want to eat any of it. The hot lasagna she'd left in the oven taunted him—*look at what domestic bliss could be like, you fool, hot cheese and meat sauce dished up to your mouth every night.*

It was too cliché. She was the little good-hearted sane person who comes in and cleans up his bachelor sty, warming his cold heart with vacuuming and hot cookies. Next thing he knew he'd be sitting down on the toilet to piss.

He shivered. He should turn on the heat but then he'd have to stand up. She must be cold. Nipples puckered up and hard, her skin covered in goose bumps. He smiled. Hopefully, her van leaked.

He managed to point the remote at his television and click on the local news. They were in for a bad storm, the kind Vegas occasionally saw this time of year. He flopped back on his bed, staring at his phone. If she was smart, she'd come here—insist on sleeping in her van in the garage or some garbage like that.

A vision of her smiling came into his mind. He'd been grumbling about luxury toilets last week and she'd started grinning. There was a gap between her top front teeth.

He grabbed his phone.

Hey, you okay?

A minute passed. He pulled the blanket up over his chest.

MAGGIE

I've been better.

What's going on?

Two minutes passed. He hated waiting. Was she messing with him?

Well, I'm having some minivan problems that's all. The battery died on me. Not sure yet what I'm going to do…I mean I can totally sleep here, not a big deal. It's just a little flooded but should be drained out in a few hours.

Chase cursed.

Where are you?

She was the slowest texter he'd ever had the misfortune of dealing with.

MAGGIE

Do you think one of your guys could run a battery out here tomorrow morning?

Half a minute after that she wrote:

I'm at Red Rock Canyon Campground.

He splashed cold water on his face. He grabbed bagged cookies and a Coke, shoving them into the pockets of his jacket. His vision blurred and he gripped the counter.

Stay where you are. I'm coming to get you.

MAGGIE PULLED the sleeping bag up higher, covering her chin. Rain battered her minivan as it rocked in an unsettling way in its deep puddle of water. She was an idiot for texting Chase not to come. At least she was an idiot with some pride. He probably couldn't stand at this point, let alone drive in a storm. She shivered, her damp hair clammy between her face and the pillow.

BAM BAM. Toto jumped up, barking and snarling. Maggie bolted upright then froze, terror washing over her. A fist had hit her window. *The tire iron!* She pulled her legs out of the sleeping bag in frantic haste, the fabric catching on her pajama pants. Her hand rummaged around in the dark, knocking over her water bottle with a clang.

"Maggie," came a familiar exasperated voice. "It's Chase. Get the fuck out here before I drown."

Maggie collapsed on her butt, heart hammering on her ribcage. After gasping in a few breaths, she unlocked the side door and slid it open.

"What's with the homicidal banging?" she said into his flashlight beam. "I thought you were a serial killer."

"Give me stuff to carry," he ordered. "The truck is on higher ground."

He hustled her and Toto into the truck. She insisted on taking the sleeping bag and air mattress which made him roll his eyes. They were both soaked by the time Chase banged her door shut. He ran around to the driver's side to jump in.

"Thank you." She watched him step up into the truck. "I want you to know I appreciate it but that it doesn't mean we're going to..." She trailed off as she got a good look at him.

The cab light showed her his haggard face, a bright red band across the bridge of his nose, his lips cracked and dry. His eyebrows were pinched together. He turned away and coughed against his shoulder.

She put her hand on his forehead. He held still with his eyes closed. She blew her breath out in a low whistle. "That's some fever. It hurts everywhere, doesn't it?" He leaned back and pressed on his forehead, not answering. "Chase," she said in her best imitation of an army sergeant, "move over. I'm driving." She reached down and unbuckled her seat belt.

Before she could get her door open the big truck revved into gear and jolted forward. Toto barked, wagging his tail.

"Nobody drives my truck but me," he said through gritted teeth. "Better buckle your seatbelt, sweetheart." His bright eyes flashed at her in the dark cab.

Thirty minutes of nerve-shattering, intense driving later, they pulled into his driveway. Neither of them had spoken much while on the highway, only glancing at abandoned cars left on the side of the road and tow trucks everywhere. He parked in the garage and collapsed forward, resting his head against the steering wheel.

She reached out and grabbed his hand, holding it firmly

in hers. He was a maniac with control issues but she still appreciated the heck out of him. "Thanks." She squeezed his fingers. "Come on, let's get you inside."

She managed to pull off his jacket before he collapsed onto his bed, boots hanging over the side. She sat down next to him and undid his laces. "When's the last time you took any painkillers?"

"Advil at lunch," he mumbled into his pillow.

"Then you're due for more. I'll be right back. Pull those jeans off and get under your sheets."

When she got back, he hadn't moved but was shivering, his whole body shaking, on top of his covers.

"Oh, my word," she said. "You're as sick as your secrets. Get up and take these—you need to get that fever down." After much coaxing, some back patting, and finally a threat to call his cousin, he sat up and swallowed the pills then collapsed back onto his bed with his eyes closed.

It took ten minutes, but she managed to work his wet jeans off while he dozed on the bed. She looked down at him lying in his underwear and a T-shirt, so uncharacteristically helpless and vulnerable. She jumped when he grabbed her hand. He yanked hard and she fell forward onto the bed next to him.

"Lie with me for a minute. I'm cold and you're so warm." The opposite was true—he burned with fever, and she was clammy and chilled. At least she had on dry clothes after changing when they had first gotten there. He put his arms around her and pulled her back against his chest, nuzzling his face into her shoulder. She blew out a long breath. *Just until he falls asleep.*

Toto jumped up on the mattress and curled up at her feet. Chase was an oven of heat, baking the tension out of her back. She sighed and relaxed her head onto his arm.

There was a tantalizing bulge pressed against her underside. Her body tingled with the awareness of him cupped around her body. His free hand reached around and held hers, keeping them clasped together on the blanket in front of her.

"I missed you," he mumbled into her hair.

"Careful," she said softly. "You'll shock me with all of this sweet stuff." He kissed her shoulder. After a moment she continued, "It's confusing."

He hugged her tighter against him then relaxed. His breathing slowed and deepened. She stayed lying against him for an hour, listening to his deep breaths and trying not to think about how good it felt to be in his arms. She was in so much trouble.

CHAPTER EIGHT

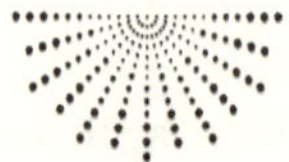

Monday afternoon, Chase dragged himself out of his truck and into the house. The prospect of Maggie bending over him all evening kept him going, even if it was only to give him medicine and force liquids down his throat. His head ached as he took off his shoes by the door. Getting over to the building site had been unavoidable that morning. Not fainting while there, or while driving, had been the tricky part.

Toto greeted him at the door with barks and a wary growl.

"Move it, rat dog." Apparently, Toto was home alone. The little terrier followed him into the house, staring at him coldly.

On the kitchen counter was a pile of pills with a sticky note next to them that said *two p.m.* Chase looked at his watch. One thirty was close enough. The note said, *get a bottle of Gatorade from the fridge.* Meekly, he walked over and pulled out a bottle of orange stuff. He poured half of the bottle down his throat along with the pills. The cold liquid was heaven.

The pulsing cloud in his head started to thin out as his brain rehydrated. "Your head hurts because your brain is thirsty," she'd said to him yesterday. The image of his dried-up shriveled brain had profoundly bothered him. After one day of her nursing, he was her whipped dog. She'd said three years of caring for her dying grandmother had taught her a thing or two and she was right. When he didn't follow her orders, he regretted it.

He crashed down onto his mattress. She'd bustled around all day yesterday, shopping, making soup, washing his sheets, baking bread, forcing a popsicle on him, sticking a thermometer into his mouth. He'd mostly slept. Her fussing had given him ample time to enjoy views of her backside as she speed walked across the family room.

When she'd set up an inflatable mattress in the downstairs bedroom, he'd grunted, "Good." Inside he'd been almost tearfully relieved. When she was with him, he was grounded, anchored in the moment of her busy activity. He liked to guess what she was cooking without looking or asking. He'd figure it out eventually by sorting out the smells and sounds: a knife on the cutting board, the clang of a pot on the stove, butter and onion sizzling, the oven door snapping shut.

He had to settle into a sexual agreement with her. They needed boundaries, roles to play. He wasn't interested in a vanilla, leave it to beaver, type of relationship. He was an emotional black pit. There wasn't any ending to how fucked up he felt—what he didn't want anyone to see.

There were so many things he'd like to do to her. He'd explore every facet of tension and chemistry between them. She was closer to giving in, he could feel it. He had to be patient a little longer. Wanting stirred in his pelvis, a deep ache of need. If his head wasn't a throbbing blister of pain, he'd be ready to nudge her along. The only thing he was currently nudging was his pillow and an ice pack.

Where was she? An hour passed, then another. Toto jumped up on the mattress next to him. He began to be put out with her. She should be here, leaning over his face to take his temperature, showing him the beautiful curves of her chest. He rolled over and pushed himself upright. Sitting on the edge of the bed, he rested his head in his hands until the dizziness cleared.

He wandered into the kitchen. In the fridge were tall cylindrical glasses layered with colored whip cream stuff and what looked like Jell-O. He ate one, the fruity sweetness coating his throat. He let Toto out to run around the fenced-in backyard. The medication was kicking in and he felt less like he was stuck swimming under water. Toto came back in and ate the pile of dog food he poured on the floor for him.

Sighing with resignation, he headed over to his computer to do more of the endless customer service for his business. There was a folded-up paper stuck under the corner of his laptop.

Chase,

it read in Maggie's handwriting.

One of the girls from Pahrump is in town today and we're going out for a girls' afternoon. I'll be back in a few hours to check on you. Can you let Toto out and then make sure he comes back in? Leftovers are in the fridge, labeled and ready for the microwave.

MAGGIE'S EYELIDS seemed glued open. She was standing on the edge of a balcony, 114 feet up somebody had said, a harness attached to a flimsy looking line. Her heart rattled in her chest. Tingles burst under her skin, radiating throughout her entire body. The roof of her mouth was tacky, her dry tongue sticking strangely to its surface. The SlotZilla Zip Line stretched in front of her, the wires like thick rope across the ceiling of the outdoor Fremont Street mall. It was a fancy carnival ride for adults—and she was about to fly.

Next to her, Princess undulated her body in a provocative imitation of pole dancing. Most of the eyes on the platform were glued to her gyrating hips and pierced belly button showing under a short halter top.

A moment ago, or maybe an hour ago, they were having coffee at the Retro Cafe, a bakery Maggie had contacted for work. Princess had been a little depressed, exhausted she said by a week of "fucking old wind bags." Now they were here, while the sun set behind the casinos, about to go on the zip line, superhero-style. Maggie swallowed, closing and opening her eyes. Nope, she really was standing on the edge of a too small ledge. She hated heights.

The huge digital screen that was the canopy over Fremont Street lit up with images of swimming fish and an underground coral reef. Remixed Elvis songs thrummed the crowd with heavy beats and deep bass. Maggie rocked her head back and forward. Don't be cruel, purred Elvis, the words like stardust popping in her veins. She could listen to this song for the rest of her life.

And then Princess pushed her and they were flying over the street, arms forward in the Superman pose. Maggie giggled and couldn't stop. The air tickled her—life was tickling her. Princess, flying on the zip line next to her, held up her shirt and flashed the crowd below them. Maggie laughed harder. Some resistant stubborn part of her was ringing an alarm bell. *Hey! Idiot! You're stoned!* She was stoned and it felt wonderful.

Gasping, tears running down her face, she was caught on the landing platform by a burly guy with tattoos down both his arms. She smiled and leaned into him, relishing the feel of his hand gripping her harness while he unclipped her. He sucked in a breath and looked intently into her eyes. She smiled up at him. Princess grabbed her and pulled her away from those intriguingly rough callused hands. Hands like Chase's.

"Not time for that yet," said Princess. "We're going clubbing."

And then they were in a candy shop called the Sugar Factory, sucking on blinged out lollipops in an empty corner of the cafe. The place was decorated with pictures of celebrities sucking on lollipops. It was strange. Maggie contemplated it, a profound realization eluding her.

"Hey," said Princess, digging around in her bag, "it's time for another dose."

"Huh?" said Maggie, staring at the glistening surface of her red lollipop.

"Time for more Sally—MDA." Princess grabbed a bag of white powder. "Dip your lollipop in this."

Maggie blinked. MDA. That was what was in her.

Princess rolled her eyes and pulled the bag back. "Like this, look," she said. She dipped the top of her lollipop, coating it in white powder.

"Wait," said Maggie, twitching from a sharp jab in her belly. Her heart pounded in her eardrums. What was MDA exactly, she couldn't remember...What the heck was happening to her? "How did I take that earlier? How much have I had?" She'd tried something like that and hadn't liked it—drugs had a strong and weird effect on her. Her chest tightened and constricted. She blew out her breath, the air stuttering from her mouth like an engine that wouldn't start.

"Relax," said Princess. "I know you're having a good time."

"Yeah, but I get to choose what goes in my body." Maggie jabbed her fingertips into her temples. "You put it in my coffee at lunch, didn't you?"

Princess shrugged. "You like it. I didn't realize you were such a pussy."

Maggie tried to keep her swirling thoughts focused. Maybe she could do this. She had taken who knew how much about two hours ago. Her vision blurred, light and shadow bouncing around, the pattern of the tiled floor jumping out, making her head whip back. "How much longer is this going to last?" she croaked.

"Oh, my gawd, you are such a baby. Come on, let's go somewhere more fun."

Maggie wanted to do something but she couldn't think of what it was. Princess towed her along like a fish on a hook. *Just let go of the worm.* Maggie smiled. She'd like to swim to a nice soft couch somewhere and lie down. And listen to Elvis.

CHASE CALLED Maggie's phone for the tenth time. No matter how much he told himself to relax, he was about as calm as a cat in a trap. It wasn't like her. Ring ring, ring ring ring. And to voice mail again. He left his third message.

A text alert dinged on his phone. It was from Maggie. He blew out a breath.

MAGGIE

Hi

Where are you? What's going on?

A minute passed.

> I'm in a bathroom. Don't feel good.

He scraped a hand over his face.

> I'm calling again. Answer your damn phone.

"Hey," a barely audible Maggie croaked. Loud music played close by and female voices talked all around her.

"Are you all right? Why the fuck haven't you said two shits to my texts or calls?"

"Umm."

What the hell was wrong with her? Was she doing another guy?

"My friend drugged me. Called it Sammy or Sally or something M…I don't know."

"What?" Chase ran a hand through his hair, making his head ache harder. Did she just say her friend drugged her?

"I'm a little confused but I think it's wearing off. She's angry with me now and doesn't want to leave. What time is it? Is Toto okay?"

Chase swallowed rage. This girl had the worst luck. "It's almost ten at night. Where are you?"

"Oh no, you should be sleeping."

"Maggie," he said with an edge in his voice, "where are you?"

"I'm not really sure. It's a club that plays a lot of Snoop Dogg. There're girls dancing inside glass boxes and in bathtubs. It seemed like heaven when we first got here and now I just really want to lie down."

"Don't lie down, Maggie. Go outside and sit by the big water fountain. I'll be there in twenty minutes." He threw two cough drops in his mouth. He wanted to lie down too.

"What if Princess gets in trouble on her own? She's stumbling around and these guys are all over her."

"Maggie, she drugged you. She's not your friend, she's a psychopath."

"Yeah, I think I'm going to be angry about this tomorrow." There was a scuffling nearby. "Oh, hey Princess," Maggie said. The phone sounded like it was put in a washing machine. There was some kind of struggle. Chase jumped in his truck.

Another voice shouted, "FUCK OFF" and the line went dead.

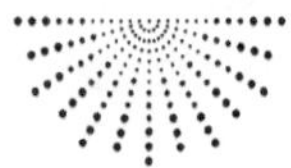

Maggie huddled over her ginger ale. Little bubbles rose to the surface and popped. There was a skinny arm slung over her shoulders. Dangling, oh so casually, on his wrist was a watch with forty diamonds on the outer ring. The bezel, he'd called it, when she'd asked if the diamonds served a purpose. Since they were right in front of her face, she'd counted them.

Cologne wafted off him in waves. She didn't like it. Princess had taken her phone and wouldn't give it back. What was it with everyone taking her dang phone? The lights and noise kept distracting her. Now she was stuck on the inside of this corner table.

It was her fault. She attracted the wrong men and the wrong friends. *Bad luck.* Maggie shuddered, gripping the stone on her necklace. Grandpa Billy had given it to her, before he died. "The best view comes after the hardest climb," he used to say to her, one of his trucker sayings.

If she wasn't so dizzy, she'd get away from the table.

Strobe lights swirled around the room, passing over their table and blinding her eyes. The guys around her tried to get her to drink again. She shook her head and pushed the shot away.

Someone stepped up to their table, their shoulders blocking a passing floodlight. Maggie looked up, blinking over her dry eyeballs.

"Hey, Maggie," said Chase. "Get the fuck out here."

She pushed against the table, rattling the glasses. She was stuck in the center of five people on the wraparound booth seat. Princess smiled an absent woozy grin. She had been taking a lot of the powder.

"Hey, man," said the guy next to her. "The lady doesn't have to go anywhere."

"No," croaked Maggie, scooting sideways, trying to force someone to budge. "He's been waiting to take me home. I need to get going, everyone. Let me out please."

She was suddenly furious with Princess. The drug had worn off a bit and her empty stomach clenched. The noise in the club made her head pound painfully.

"What are you, some kind of abusive boyfriend?" The guy next to her put his hand under the table and gripped her thigh. Maggie gasped.

Chase grabbed the table and yanked it backward, sliding the wooden slab a few feet. Everyone's drinks fell over. The guys jumped to their feet, spluttering and cursing. Maggie pushed her way past them. She grabbed Princess's purse off the bench and pulled out her phone. Chase took her hand. She dropped the purse on the floor.

A security guard appeared next to them. "You all got a problem over here?"

"This fucker just grabbed our table," sneered one guy. He wiped the front of his trousers with a napkin.

Chase shrugged. "We're leaving," he said. They walked away, holding hands.

~

MAGGIE BLINKED, fighting the sensation that she was floating outside her body. They were in a very upscale Asian restaurant and club, with multiple levels, a swimming pool patio outside, and a giant two-story-tall Buddha statue on the main floor. The statue's eyes were closed, an expression of bliss on its massive face. People danced, red fabric waved, loud music pounded, and screens flashed. She had a meat pounder smashing her brain. It was fried.

Chase pulled her along at a fast clip, his grip on her hand hard. He jostled, pushed and intimidated people into shifting over. She wanted to close her eyes and ride out of there curled up on his shoulder, a sleepy little parrot holding on to him with her talons. She shook her head, trying to clear her fuzzy vision. Whatever the drug "Sally" was, she'd had an intense reaction to it.

Finally, they were passing through the long entryway, made of horseshoe arches separated by bathtubs. There were a couple of girls in the tubs, twirling their feet around in the air, rose petals strategically covering their pink bits. Weren't they cold? Maggie shivered as brisk air hit them in the large columned shopping mall they stepped into. It was all gold and marble and skinny mannequins. Her heels clicked loudly in her ears. Her stomach really hurt.

A pink-haired person tried to hand them a flier. Chase ignored it, not slowing down. Maggie would have looked over her shoulder to apologize, or at least shrug, but was afraid she'd trip. A gondola passed by on the interior waterway, a couple snuggled up in the rear of the boat. When had she ever done anything even remotely like that? The heavy sadness that had been creeping up on her for the last few hours settled over her like a cloak.

They stepped outside into the cold, clear night. Loud

traffic cruised by them on the strip. A party bus shook as it rumbled by, hip-hop blasting from its speakers.

"Wait." Maggie pulled her hand out of his. "Got to breathe for a second." She leaned against a railing.

Chase pushed his fingers through his hair. The vein under his right eye did a pulsing thing. He walked in a tight circle and stopped in front of her, very close.

"Why the hell didn't you call me sooner?" he said through gritted teeth.

"Um." Maggie blinked. "That stuff scrambled my brain. Two and two made zero, you know?"

"What the hell is this?" He gestured at her clothing.

"I'm not sure." Maggie pulled the shimmering gold halter top down a little. The top didn't even come close to meeting the fringed leather mini skirt. "Princess pulled me into a shop and bought it."

Chase stared at her like she was dirt.

"It's embarrassing." Maggie kept her eyes on his ear. She liked how the tips flopped down a little. "I mean, this is the second time you've rescued me this week. You're my employer. Calling for a party save is awkward."

"I'm more than your employer." He yanked her forward and put his arms around her. "You scared the shit out of me." He smelled like cough drops and Chase, sweaty and salty. Her body responded before her brain could process what was happening. She wrapped her arms around his back, her face nuzzling into his shoulder. She'd wanted to do this for so long.

He grunted, resting his head on top of hers. Then he started coughing. She stepped away and patted his back. Her face scrunched up—she really should have been able to handle everything on her own. His cough subsided slowly. He closed his eyes.

"That makes me feel horrible, seeing you out here sick."

"Good." He grabbed her hand.

They walked for another ten minutes before they got to his truck parked in a pay garage. Her mind was dredging up stuff she'd avoided thinking about. Some of the worst moments of her childhood. Like when she was eight, shy and tense, and her mother had disappeared. For years, while living with her grandparents, loving as they had been, she'd waited for sights of her mother and for the time when she'd finally love her enough to come get her. But she never had. Maggie had decided she was worthless—not even her mother wanted her. It wasn't until her Grandpa Billy had started cooking with her that the sadness had loosened. Somehow, she was back to missing her mother in her head as she trudged down the crowded noisy Vegas strip with Chase. Worthless, always making mistakes, forever the girl that got thrown away.

Chase's truck beeped. Maggie shook her head to clear her thoughts, startled by the sight of his haggard face under the fluorescent lights of the parking garage. He opened her door, staring at her like she was a problem. That was her.

"You didn't have to come get me," she said to him as she pulled the seatbelt over her chest. "I could have taken a cab."

He slammed her door shut and got in on the driver's side. The engine started. "Right," he said, sarcastically. "Just as soon as you got away from your gang rape."

"I was sitting at a bar table, not locked up in a dungeon." She fumbled for her Djucu-nut necklace and clutched it.

"You were in a fucking lot of trouble," he snapped. He took a corner too fast. Maggie gripped the "oh crud" handle above her seat. She shouldn't argue with him while he was driving. Whatever that drug had done to her brain was affecting her ability to keep her mouth shut.

"I think it's only fair to tell you that I'm hoping to have another job in the next couple weeks."

"Fine," he ground out. "If you find something that pays better, by all means go shake your tail somewhere else."

"Tail shaking is not involved, a-hole."

"Is that why you were partying all night with a sex worker and a bunch of rich dicks? Don't lie to me, Maggie."

"That twisted story in your head is not what happened to me. I'm applying for jobs in professional kitchens and bakeries, you idiot."

He huffed but didn't say anything, his jaw tense. She closed her eyes and focused on breathing. It didn't matter what he thought of her, she told herself. In fact, it was better when they were fighting.

"I was worried." He took a deep breath.

Maggie swallowed around the lump in her throat. She gasped, blinking her burning eyes.

"I didn't want you to see me like this. I thought I could handle it…" She leaned forward, putting her face in her hands.

"Shh," Chase said, squeezing her knee. He pulled her sideways until her head rested on his thigh, her tears puddling on his jeans. She covered her eyes with her arm.

"You're feeling the comedown from the MDA and it can be brutal. They're trying to use that stuff to treat PTSD, but the crash isn't worth the high. Hang in there, you'll feel better tomorrow. And back to normal by the day after." He sniffed. "Probably."

CHASE GOT Maggie into the house. She was still sniffling and he hated it. Toto whined, frantically wagging his tail, and jumped up on his hind legs. Maggie crouched down and hugged him, burying her face in his fur.

Thankfully, for his peace of mind, her van was still in the

shop where he'd had it towed, so she wouldn't be trying to drive off anywhere tonight in a fit of self-destructive madness. He pulled her into the kitchen where he plunked her down on a chair. Toto jumped up on her lap.

"I'm going to set you up in the family room for the night, on my mattress," he said. She stiffened. "You'll probably have a hard time sleeping. Relax, I'll grab my sheets and sleep on the air mattress in the other room. Make some tea and get into your pajamas. With the ugly penguins on them."

She wiped her face and sniffed, a half-smile appearing on her face. Something stirred in his chest. This damn girl was so much trouble, especially when she was trying not to be.

He got the bedding switched around while she fed Toto then changed. She emerged, face scrubbed of makeup, looking pale and way too young for what he wanted to do to her. What he would do to her as soon as he wasn't feverish with a burning sore throat. And she wasn't doped up.

He yawned, shuffling his schedule in his head so he could survive the workday. Maggie turned down the lights then sat on the chair. Frowning, she picked at a piece of spice bread she'd made that morning.

"Try to relax," he said, "and not let your brain go down dark rabbit holes." He clicked on the television. After a minute of not liking what he saw on the premium channels he switched over to on demand. *The Goonies* started, that old upbeat Cindy Lauper song playing.

"Wow," she said flatly, "this is a movie from ancient times."

Chase grinned, relieved to hear the old Maggie for a moment. "*The Goonies* is the best thing that happened in the eighties." He angled the TV so it faced his bed. The bed that now had her sleeping bag on it.

She padded over and lay down on top of the bedding,

curled up on her side. He wanted to spoon around her and sink his face into those blonde curls.

Instead, he turned off the hallway light and dragged himself to an uncomfortable air mattress, his feet hanging off the end. He sighed, disgusted with himself. Once he started sleeping with her, he'd get this all out of his system, whatever the hell it was. It would just be sex, and only sex. And damn good sex.

Five hours later he woke up and checked on her. She was asleep on top of the sleeping bag. He turned off the television then covered her up. At least he wasn't a total monster, when it came to Maggie.

CHAPTER TEN

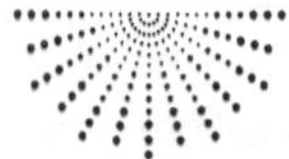

Maggie jumped down from the van onto the hot asphalt of the cheapest gas station in town. Her vision swam. She reached out a hand to lean on the warm side of the mini. Vegas weather in the winter was all over the place but today there was seventy-degree heat and bright pounding sunlight.

The gas nozzle dripped as she dragged it over to the filler hole. The numbers ticked up on the register as her money flushed down into the minivan's eleven-gallon tank.

She opened the side door and sat down in the doorway. Toto jumped out and sniffed around the garbage can. She'd just vacuumed the ancient, flattened carpet but it was still stained and matted. Repairing the minivan had eaten up half of her first week's earnings. She'd be camping for a while longer. She put Toto back in the mini and closed the doors.

That morning she'd gotten up in time to fix Chase's breakfast, pack his lunch, and fill his canteen with coffee. He'd interrupted her rambling about his schedule when he'd walked over and held her face in both hands. They'd stared into each other's eyes. "You okay?" he'd asked.

"Yeah," she'd lied, not able to force a smile. Slowly he'd leaned forward, dark eyebrows drawn together. He'd rubbed her nose with his. She'd huffed, her chest tight.

"See you tonight," he'd said and walked out.

Maggie walked into the minimart and stood at the end of the long line to pay for her gas with cash. The thing that was happening between her and Chase was all wrong. She wanted to meet someone who saw her at her best—with a career and a nice apartment, not living in her van. Chase could never have serious feelings for her, not when he'd met her in a brothel.

A text from him popped up on her phone screen.

CHASE

I'm home where are you?

The fatal thing was, she'd started to think his version of the future might happen. Not because she was giving in to his coercion—darn him. No, it wasn't that he stubbornly, mulishly, didn't give up. The problem was she'd never wanted anyone so much in her life. It wouldn't last, but goodness, could she live her entire life without having a few weeks with him to remember? She stepped up to the counter and handed over her money.

Back in the minivan, she slumped in her seat, staring at her phone, not sure what she wanted to say to him. The drug hangover made her weak. *Pull it together.* Sleeping with him would be like an atomic bomb in her unstable tenuous life. The fallout would be toxic. If she was stronger, richer, had a network of friends and family, she could see herself being a person that sought out that kind of excitement. She sighed.

Back to the campsite. Any requests for meals this week?

CHASE

Don't do this. Come back. I'm not going to force anything on you.

She massaged her aching head. *Yeah right.* He only wanted to force a sexual contract on her.

I need the desert air to clear my head tonight. And I have jobs to apply to.

You're not safe driving around in that old clunker. Come back. Let me take you out to dinner.

Watch out, that sounds like dating. A relationship. The normal kind.

You know that's not what I can offer. In some ways what we'll have will be better. More honest.

Maggie pressed on her tight chest, a little sick to have it confirmed again. He hadn't budged an inch. He wanted to define their relationship around sex and that was it. It hurt.

Sorry, I can't do the sex only thing. It would make me feel even more worthless than I already do.

She blew out her breath slowly, finger hovering over the send button, and then jabbed quickly down before she could change her mind.

He didn't respond. She swallowed down some water and started the engine of her old clunker.

CHASE PULLED off his hard hat. His part of the project was finished on time. *Barely.* The new development in Summerlin was a gold star on his resume. He didn't give a shit.

Jose rolled up next to him in his truck. "Hey, boss," he said, leaning out of the open window. "What you doin', man? You got a hot date tonight?"

Johnny bent forward in the seat next to Jose. "Dude, we met the blonde working for you last week." Johnny shook his hand as if it was burned then bit his knuckle. "Stole that little sugar pie from the Dirty Rabbit, didn't ya?"

"She never really worked there." Chase forced down a bolt of anger that the guys would bring that up. "I was her first and only customer."

"She your girlfriend now?" asked Jose.

Girlfriend. He hadn't introduced anyone as his girlfriend in a while. "Yeah," he said slowly, "she is."

Jose whistled. "And she cooks too. Damn. You should invite us over—I saw that pool in your backyard. You gotta have a barbecue when you have a pool like that."

Girlfriend, Chase thought on the drive home. And a barbecue with friends. Maggie would like that.

It had been a miserable week. He'd been working long hours wrapping up the Summerlin project while fighting off the damn flu. Maggie had been avoiding him. He'd scarcely seen her, too busy in the mornings to do more than stare at her while she talked at him. At night she was gone. He got home, ate what she'd left him, drank a beer and crashed.

He was drinking less. A lot less. The flu and his withdrawal from the intensive drinking were happening at the same time. It was painful but a lot easier than he deserved.

That damn campground wasn't far. He would go out there and talk to her. And more.

The sun was out and it was technically still afternoon. He

smiled. Tonight, he finally had some time. He turned the corner onto his street and his house came into view. There were cars jammed into the driveway and parked along both sides of the street. He clenched his teeth, the vein pulsing under his eye.

~

MAGGIE BIT HER BOTTOM LIP, watching Lucas slowly move his hand away from the cupcake balanced on his head. His girlfriend giggled and wiggled her toes. Her long legs were sticking straight up from where she lay on the ground next to the pool, heels balanced against Lucas's belly, two cupcakes on the bottoms of her feet. Two people hid behind Lucas with their arms fanned out around him, each hand holding a cupcake. Maggie placed two more cupcakes in Lucas's hands and backed away, holding her breath.

"We've got it." She depressed the shutter button, taking multiple shots, capturing the changing expression on Lucas's face. It was an imitation of the multi-armed Asian statue, one of the Hindu gods she'd seen at the fancy club she'd been at with Princess.

The cupcake slid off Lucas's head and landed on his girl-friend's tummy. She squealed, her feet twitching. Lucas took bites out of any cupcakes close to his mouth.

"Ahh," said Maggie in a bad French accent, "your improvisation is a beautiful thing."

A door slammed somewhere. *Uh-oh.* Maggie took pictures of the cupcake tower she'd created on a table, while she still could. Bathing-suit-clad college kids milled around in the background of her photo frame, among the palm trees and in the blue water of the swimming pool. She focused on the cupcakes with a shallow depth of field so that the people would be blurry, soft, and out of focus. Two years as the yearbook photographer at her high school had taught her how to use a camera.

She needed to kick all these people out and clean up. She forced herself to stop taking pictures. She had no idea what time it was.

The music abruptly stopped. Lucas looked up from licking frosting off a cupcake on his girlfriend's chest. Maggie whirled around.

"You have ten fucking minutes to get off my property," Chase yelled with his hands cupped around his mouth. Everyone froze. "Anyone still here after that will be charged with trespassing. Leave any trash, assholes, and I'll shove it down your throat. Move it, people. Clock starts now."

The people moved. Maggie glanced at Lucas and he shrugged and winked, shoving the rest of a cupcake into his mouth. People streamed out of the side gate, congregating in the small park on the other side of the back fence. A girl darted in, looking for a cell phone while Chase glared at her. He slammed the gate behind her as she ran out, eyes big. He stomped off into the house. There was shouting on the second story and more slamming doors.

Maggie grabbed an empty box and picked up the last of the beer cans and trash around the pool. Toto barked from inside the house where she'd locked him in with a bone to chew on. Car engines were turned on in the street and driveway. The laughing crowd in the park moved off, probably to another party. Maggie sighed. Those kids had no idea how good they had it.

She was transferring her cupcakes to a tray when Chase stomped up to her. She kept moving, not looking at him.

"Maggie," he said in a tight voice, "I'm not paying you to have pool parties with a bunch of asshole frat guys."

She sighed, moving the cupcakes apart so the frosting stayed pretty. She owed him an explanation—she definitely did. The house was his property. It was just that his uptight hair-trigger temper was getting on her last nerve. She blew out a breath.

"I know that." She looked at his tight face a moment. A flood of warmth flowed into her nether regions while her heart beat an excited staccato in her chest. He was way too handsome for his own good. "Your cousin is a force of nature. He showed up this afternoon with a couple of friends. To say hi, he said." She snorted. "What a twisty weasel. Before I knew it, he'd let all those people in through the side gate. I made him clean out the pool at least."

He swung his arm out sharply, knocking the cupcakes off the table. "You should have fucking called me!"

Maggie snapped. She lunged forward and pushed him hard in the chest. His arms windmilled but he was too off balance and crashed backward into the water. There was a satisfying splash over the rim of the pool onto her bare feet. She smiled down at him as he shot up, spitting water out of his mouth.

"You can deduct today out of my salary," she called down to him. "I'm leaving."

CHAPTER ELEVEN

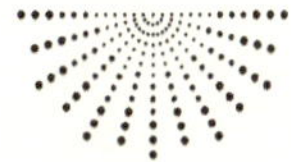

Chase hit the water and rage exploded in his chest. The pool closed over his head. The chlorinated water flooded his injured arm and burned. He squinted up at the brightness above him as his body sank to the bottom, watching bubbles from his mouth rise. He shot right back out of the water and spat out a mouthful.

There she was, picking up the cupcakes he'd knocked over, shouting down at him something about deducting from her salary and, "I'm leaving."

She hunched over, one too-skinny arm reaching down to pick up the mess he'd made. He eased back down into the water.

The monstrous rage swept out of him. The cool buoyant water eased the muscular aches in his body and the tight painful joints that dogged him since he'd cut back on drinking. He didn't want her to leave.

He pulled himself out of the pool onto a low stone bench. One of the palm trees filtered light through its fronds, casting a shadow like a hand touching the water.

The men of his platoon squad in Afghanistan had understood his rages, they'd known he would do whatever it took, including ripping them new assholes, to keep them safe. When he hadn't been able to do that, the rages had gotten worse. Until he'd come home, to civilian life, and there hadn't been anywhere "appropriate" for his rages anymore.

He pulled off his boots and sopping wet socks. Maggie ignored him, moving everything from the party back to the kitchen. Now that he was looking, he realized that the backyard was immaculately groomed, the stone surfaces clean, the tiki-themed statuary gleaming. Maggie had done a total backyard spit shine.

He pulled off his shirt, peeling the sleeve slowly down his left arm. He grunted involuntarily as the bandage pulled away from the cut over his bicep.

"You're hurt." Maggie bustled toward him with a first aid box. "I saw the kit out this morning and have been wondering what happened." She tsk tsked, bending over close to his side and spraying the cut with Bactine then dabbing gently with sterile gauze padding. There wasn't anyone else he'd want touching him. *Makes this easier.*

"Maggie." He grabbed her hand. "I shouldn't have shouted. I'm sorry—about the cupcakes too." He squeezed her hand, staring at her averted face. "Did I scare you?"

She huffed. "I should be scared," she said. She turned and looked into his eyes. "For some stupid reason I'm not."

He buried his face in her stomach, breathing in that sugary frosting smell that clung to her. A gentle hand pushed through his wet hair. He gasped, his eyes burning. What the hell was wrong with him?

She crouched in front of him and took his face in her hands, her fingers smoothing over his cheekbones. "I'm not scared of you. You're a good man, Chase Montgomery, no matter what the crazy clockwork in your head has you thinking about that."

"I'm not," he said, a fucking tear slipping down his cheek.

"You are. I'm sure of it. You're also an ornery a-hole but that can't be helped."

He grabbed her, pulling her down onto his lap. She landed on his soggy jeans, her feet splashing into the pool water. "Stay," he practically begged. "Please. Stay with me. I need to talk to you…" Her skin was too distracting, smooth, a little mole on her right shoulder.

"Yeah," she said breathlessly, "I've noticed you're a big talker."

She wasn't running away yet. He took a deep breath, willing the blood back into his brain. He suddenly realized she was wearing a bikini underneath the little dress thingy. He shivered, blowing out an unsteady breath. It's not any different from a bra and panties, he told himself as his shaky fingers traced the line of string around her neck. But somehow it was. Fucking hell, it was.

"Girlfriend," he blurted out against the side of her neck. Wow, he had to do better than that.

She stiffened up in his arms.

"Be my girl, Maggie."

He held on to her, terrified she would say no.

"You don't do the relationship thing, remember?"

"I'm no good at it. But I want to try, maybe even grow into a real human."

She was silent, a wide-eyed expression on her face. Stiff arms pulled away from his shoulders.

His stomach dropped into his ass. She was going to say no.

MAGGIE PUSHED AWAY FROM CHASE, his fingers sliding down her arm to grip her hands until she broke that contact too.

She couldn't think—she had to think. In a fog, she walked away from him and pointed herself at the pink and orange sunset sky. Heat crept all over her tingling skin as sweat broke out on her forehead. This wasn't familiar territory, what had just happened between them. She was lost, and paralyzed by a sudden avalanche of desire, confusion, hope. No, despair. It wouldn't work.

Chase shuffled around behind her. She heard wet fabric drop on the ground.

"How can you want me?" She forced herself to speak, digging her fingernails into the palms of her hands. The movement behind her stopped. She was going to make a complete fool of herself. "How can you want a relationship with me when I'm such a mess? I mean, if you ever wanted to stay at my place, don't expect to be able to stand up inside."

She flinched when he put his hands on her arms. He turned her around to face him. "How can I want you?" he repeated, a dumbstruck expression on his face. "I've never wanted anyone under me more."

She huffed, looking away.

He shook her a little. "I mean, yeah, you're a boatload of trouble at times. Maggie..." He trailed off, his eyebrows pinched together. *He's emotionally constipated.* Despite herself, her mouth quirked up.

The amusement faded. Men wanted to sleep with her, they had since she was twelve years old—or at least that's when she'd noticed it. For the first three months of fifth grade, a few older boys had forced their hands on her during her walk home from the bus stop. She'd fought them off but hadn't ever been the same after. Then Granny had waited for them with a shotgun, Grandpa Billy in his wheelchair beside her. She didn't see those boys again until after Christmas.

"Maggie," Chase said again, staring into her eyes. "Even as turned on and frustrated as I've been, I can't wait to see you. You're the best part of my day." He crouched so that their eyes were level. "You make me happy."

His rare smile transformed his face. He stared at her like a pirate stealing a treasure chest, sly and mischievous. His eyes, though, were warm. The corners of her mouth quirked up. She turned fully toward him, took a deep breath, and walked into his arms.

He groaned, lifting her up off the ground, locking her against his hard chest. She wrapped her legs around his waist. They held each other fiercely, both panting. Maggie shivered. His wet jeans were lying in a pile on the stones, and she could feel all of him through his boxers. He was long and hard against her middle, shaking a little with what might be restrained desire.

Liquid heat pooled low in her pelvis, everything between her legs swollen and hot. She reached up and pulled his mouth down to hers, ready for what came next. Their mouths clung together, tongues tasting and sliding through lips. Her breasts were tight, the nipples firm and tingling as they pressed against his wet chest.

The rushing in her ears matched the drumming of her heart, all of her focused and impatient with waiting. Pushing her center against him, she gasped, her nub grinding, coiled and pulsing. He moaned, gripping her behind and pulling her up harder.

Abruptly, he put her on her feet. She stood, dizzy, frustrated, her breath ragged. He crouched over his jeans and dug out a small square packet from the back pocket. A condom—good grief, he had a condom in his work jeans. She would think about that later.

He swooped her up into his arms, kissing her hard on the mouth. The kiss became lingering as he tasted her lips. She sucked hard on his tongue and his body jerked. He pulled his mouth away, his eyes narrowed, his face flushed, and carried her into the tiki hut.

Inside was a dark cool depression, a well in the center for the bartender to stand in. He set her down onto the stone bar, bunching her swim dress up around her hips. She looked around a little frantically but the thick grass roof hung low down the sides, protecting them from the sight of the tall houses beyond the backyard fence.

He ran his hands over her, focusing on her tight aching breasts. She swallowed, gripping the edge of the counter, struggling to sit up. He dropped to his knees and pulled her aching slit toward his face. She shuddered as his hot mouth covered the fabric over her crotch. With impatient tugs, he pulled at the strings holding her bikini together until the bow loosened and fell away. Cool air washed over her throbbing folds. She sucked in a breath, shocked at how wet she was, at his mouth closing over her. He groaned—a sound of satisfaction and hunger.

High-pitched urgent moans came from her throat. It was all she could do not to scream as a wave of release washed over her, a surge of fire rushing up into her stomach and chest. The foil packet ripped and then he was moving her legs wider apart. He jerked forward and filled her in one thrust. She leaned her head back and groaned. He pumped into her, hitting a pulsing center deep inside. She let go of the stone counter and wrapped her arms around his neck, holding on as he rode her, whimpers of ecstasy huffing out on her breath as another wave of release took her. His body shook, his rhythm sharpened and then he pushed hard into her, his hands gripping her down onto his pulsing shaft. He moaned and shivered against her.

～

RELUCTANTLY, Chase pulled out of her trembling body. He kissed her soft parted lips, open and pliant under his mouth. He quaked. *Damn.* Too much heat, too much beautiful, her body had arched into his every touch. He pulled off the condom, still trembling a little.

Her hands covered her face. He froze. "Maggie…did I hurt you?" Cold dread tightened his back.

She peeked out at him from between her fingers. His shoulders relaxed a fraction. "No, I'm fine. Shyness attack—stop looking."

With a mock growl he swooped her off the stone counter and dove his face into her neck. He could live on her giggles. "Well, I like it from behind, really like it, but talking to your unbelievably perfect ass might have its limits."

"I'm not going to make the obvious fart joke that comment deserves," she said primly, bright red and still not looking at him.

He grinned. He was absurdly happy. She wasn't going to run away even if he had to tie her to the bed. He sucked a breath in through his nose. *Slow down.*

He carried her across the little wooden bridge to the stone patio connected to the house, paused to grab a cupcake, and took a huge bite. She had her eyes down. He smeared frosting on her lips and then licked it off, kissing the corners of her mouth until they turned up.

"The neighbors definitely heard you screaming," he said, matter-of-factly.

She ducked her head into his shoulder. "I was not scream-ing." She punched his uninjured arm. He grunted, pretending to stagger under her weight. When she tried to wiggle out of his hold, he pressed her against the wall of the house and kissed her soundly. With a somewhat painful shift, he had her legs around his hips. He didn't care how much his injured arm protested, he wasn't going to let her get an inch away from him.

When he hoisted her up over his shoulder in a fireman's carry, she grunted a laugh. "Let me down, beast."

"I'm doing you a favor," he managed to say in an imitation of his normal voice. The pain made him a little breathless. He would start lifting again. "Now you don't have to look at my face." He slapped her ass. Then his hand lingered over the round curves, exploring as his cock hardened.

"You're going to regret this. You have to sleep sometime." She squirmed, panting. Hell, what had he done to deserve this? Joy rippled through him. He'd connected to her in a way that surpassed the joining of their bodies. Thinking about it made his heart stutter in his chest.

He made it into the bathroom and kicked the door shut behind him. In the mirror, she was ass-up over his shoulder and he paused to enjoy the sight of his fingers tickling between her legs. "Chase," she protested, "my head is spinning."

Relenting, he slid her down his body. Then he captured her mouth in a fierce kiss. He was wild for her again, his cock slapping against his belly, tall and proud and fucking ready for more action. She sank into him, melting against his chest. It drove him over the edge.

He dropped down in front of her and ravaged her clitoris with his mouth, sucking hard while she panted above him. Two fingers slid inside, her folds wet and swollen. He burned for her, desire so hot he was dizzy and mad with it. He yanked open a cabinet and pulled out the box of condoms he'd stashed there last week.

"You're ready," she gasped out.

"I've been thinking about this nonstop for the last two weeks."

He ripped open the packet and slid the sheath on, glad it

might slow him down. He put his hands on both sides of her face, darted in for a quick kiss, and then forced her to look at him. Her bright blue eyes were glazed and heavy lidded, her lips red and full. He smiled at her. Her eyelashes fluttered.

"You're so beautiful it kills me sometimes," he said. His eyes slid away. "I want you to hold on tight to the edge of the tub." She looked back, her mouth opening, her eyes wide. He grinned and kissed her again. "Tell me if I'm too rough. Promise?" She nodded.

He positioned her, hands braced on the side of the tub, legs spread wide. Bent over in a V, with her hips arched up, her sex was revealed in all its throbbing glory. His hands shook as he probed with his fingers, swirling the moisture out onto her folds. Then slowly, agonizingly, he sank into her. She groaned, her back arching, her hips pushing against him. He thrust up and down, gyrating in short pulses, loving her impatient wild rubbing against him.

"Chase!" she yelled. He thrust into her. She screamed, her head arching back, her sex spasming around him. He pumped into her, lost in the sight of her naked and bent over in front of him, the killing pleasure building to a nuclear pitch before he shot off inside her, his hands pulling her hips against his. She moaned, sliding up and down against him in another wet glide.

He sat down on the floor, pulling her into his lap. She sprawled against his chest, boneless, half asleep. He kissed her head, her ear, her eyebrow.

"You've done it now," she muttered then yawned against his chest. "I'm mush."

"I've just gotten started," he said, smiling as she tensed. "We came in here to shower. Until you distracted me."

"Me," she squeaked. "I was beating on your back with my fists."

He kissed her neck, biting gently under her ear. "You know how to torture me so good, vixen."

"I need food," she said. "Otherwise, you're going to be poking a puddle on the ground."

"God, you turn me on," he growled, cupping her breasts and pinching her nipple hard enough to make her gasp.

She pushed away from him and got to her feet, legs wobbling. "I'm taking a lightning-fast shower and then going to the kitchen. To eat." She emphasized the last word with a saucy glare over her shoulder.

He followed her into the shower and fondled her into another shaky orgasm. She retaliated with her hands and then, *oh hell yes*, mouth. When they staggered out, he felt drunk, even giggly, for fuck's sake. Surely it wasn't real. He'd have to end it at some point, before he got carried away.

CHAPTER TWELVE

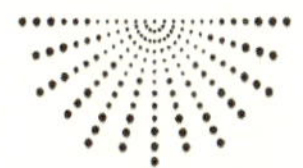

Maggie walked next to Chase into a wonderland of massive glass cube chandeliers and open steel kitchens. She froze as saliva formed on the roof of her mouth. Her eyes wouldn't settle, darting from table to table, trying to take it all in. Light reflected through a layered glass partition wall made up of transparent overlapping cubes, the colors of the desert shimmering in veins stretched throughout the sparkling surfaces.

Chase put an arm around her waist. "We have express passes, so we'll skip the lines."

She closed her eyes and put her face on his shoulder. "It's too much. There's so many—I want to try everything, but I have to be able to walk…"

He nibbled on her ear. "You'll be doing more than walking."

Grabbing his shirt in both fists, she looked into his face a little desperately. "How long can we stay? The website says five hundred dishes."

He leaned in and brushed his lips against hers. "When you pass out, or throw up, they'll probably kick us out." Gently he turned her toward one of the nine show kitchens and took her hand. "Let's walk over here and take a look. I want to try that Japanese beef."

"Wagyu," she said absently, her eyes snagging on the thousands of clear glass jars lined up on high shelves above the cooking stations. She wasn't even looking at the food yet—she was too dizzy.

"Seventeen mill to build this place," said Chase. "Brought in a hotshot design firm from Japan. It's out of step with the Roman theme of Caesar's but right in line with the excess." He sniffed. "Now everyone wants modern exposed glass, wood, and steel interiors. The work can't get done fast enough. Except some of these big projects tank and then they try to take it out on the contractors that wrap up their own budgets in labor and supplies."

Maggie studied him out of the corner of her eye. Last night and this morning he had been relaxed, affectionate and almost chatty. She took a small white plate with three red velvet pancakes piled on top, strawberry and cream sauce melting over their steaming sides. A little, okay A LOT, of sex had sweetened him right up.

Their time together had become…hedonistic. Blissful. She'd never experienced anything even remotely like it. She was sore in a way that released burning pangs of pleasure as she walked. Or sat down. Or looked too long at the way his jeans were slung low on his hips and his wide shoulders stretched his T-shirt. And his eyes, oh Sweet Jesus, he could get her uncomfortably steamy with a hard glance from between those spiky lashes. Could people look at them and tell they were a couple of oversexed maniacs? They weren't fit for public.

Crab avocado toast and truffle deviled eggs was her nod to a healthy breakfast. She took a glass bottle of fresh watermelon juice off a table of ice. Half of her tray was still empty.

She faced the pastry and dessert table. Everything from pastel macarons to precisely layered parfaits of deep purple, red, and white were laid out in lines. She reached out to take a pignolo cookie, almond paste and golden pine nuts decorating its top, and then pulled her hand back. There were canelé—like flower-shaped waterfalls frozen in time, their Bundt shapes filled with custard in the center and sealed with a caramel crust exterior. And she couldn't forget about the chocolate-dipped eclairs, custard stuffed lobster tails, pink and red mini-mousse cakes, raspberry tarts, and delicate mille-feuille—their tops marbleized in white and dark chocolate.

People were walking past her, looking back over their shoulders with raised eyebrows. If they had car horns, they'd be honking.

Chase came up next to her with an empty tray. He started piling on a massive variety. She murmured in alarm and grabbed his arm. "What are you doing? We can't eat all that."

"It's research." He winked at her. He took her healthy breakfast tray from her and handed her the one half-full of pastries. "I'll get coffee."

Giving in to his evil persuasion, she filled the tray, knocking on wood whenever she could to dispel the bad luck from wasting so much. She transferred the plates onto a table, grouping the pastry by type. Chase, a grin on his face, set down her coffee and a mini pitcher of cream.

"I think we should pray for forgiveness. And digestion," said Maggie.

"This is Sin City, we're a lost cause." He cut into a long piece of bacon. "Besides, it's New Years. What the hell is that frothy looking pink cake? It reminds me of fiberglass insulation."

"Milhoja," said Maggie, cutting into the flaky interior with her fork. "It's Argentinian, made of stacked layers of puff pastry, filled with silky dulce de leche cream and topped with Italian meringue. I've been dying to try one." She stuck the fork in her mouth and closed her eyes in pleasure, groaning softly.

Chase cleared his throat. He was flushed and staring at her mouth. She smiled, glad she wasn't the only one having dirty thoughts. She'd like to eat this cake off his stomach…

"Whatever you're thinking, stop." He pinned her ankles with his legs under the table. "Hard-ons screw with my digestion."

"Here, try this." She held out the fork.

"No thank you, dear, I don't eat anything that color of pink. Don't make the pouty face. Fine." He took her fork in his mouth and his lips closed firmly over the tines. He shut his eyes and moaned. Loudly.

"Chase," she hissed, her face roasting. People were looking at them.

"Let's go back to bed. We'll come here another time."

"Not a chance."

She didn't force any more insulation-colored food on him, and they settled into serious eating. Their table had a view of a decadently long swimming pool, one of many, surrounded by tall columns and replicated Roman statuary. It was the most sumptuous meal she'd ever had. She was afraid to tell him so—to lay out what a dirt-poor upbringing she'd had. He'd moved around the expensive restaurant setting like he was a normal part of the scenery, extravagant buffets a mild weekend diversion.

Tasting everything turned out to be an overwhelming challenge. It had been a strategic mistake to eat the red velvet pancakes. Maggie leaned back, sipping her third cup of coffee.

"How about a hike?" she said. "Otherwise, I'll need a hot water bottle for my tummy."

"I bought us tickets for the roller-coaster ride on top of the Stratosphere," Chase said.

Maggie blinked at him. "That could get pretty ugly. You're joking, aren't you?" She looked at him from between her fingers. He kept an expression of innocent bewilderment on his face. She swallowed. "Heights aren't my favorite thing in the world."

His face relaxed into a crooked grin. "A hike sounds fine. And the weather's good for it." He took a sip of coffee. "First, we'll make a sex pit stop at home. Those oysters are revving my engine, babe."

"Nope. I see through your evil plan. If we go to the house, you'll want to nap all afternoon and I won't be able to walk. You promised whatever I wanted today and you will deliver, sir."

"Hmm," he crooned, "I love it when you call me sir."

She ignored that, keeping her focus firmly on the crumb-covered plates in front of her. If they didn't stop with all the flirting, she'd never bring up what was on her mind. She smoothed her hand over the table.

"I think we should talk about a few things," she said lamely. Good grief, she was such a coward.

"What's on your mind, dumplin'?"

"Dumplin'? No no, not dumplin'. Stop distracting me."

"I'm listening, my little pastry puff."

"Chase." Maggie sat up straighter. "All right, hush, let me talk. Well, I'm a worrier—I mean, I am when I stop to think. Anyway, I'm wondering how things are going to change now that we're, you know, stuffing the donut together, so to speak…"

Chase choked on his coffee, bending over.

"Nothing wrong with a polite term here and there." She crossed her arms.

He sat up, his eyes twinkling. "Sustained." He tapped the

table for a moment, staring at her. "The biggest change is you won't be sleepin' in that predator-bait minivan anymore. If you try, I'll follow you and keep you up all night complaining about my cramped legs. And stuffin' the donut until the floor falls through."

Maggie sighed. "Your threats are terrifying." She folded her napkin then pulled it apart again. "But really—you want me there, in your house, all the time? I'm not sure we're ready for that. It's too fast. But it's going to be a couple more weeks before I can afford my own place..."

"Hey." He reached across the table and grabbed her hand. "I do want you there all the time. Definitely. It's gonna be great. Stop worrying."

"So, I'll take the den off the main entrance since the upstairs isn't finished."

"You'll put your stuff in there and sleep with me. Hell, maybe we should both sleep in there. I might do somethin' extravagant, like buy a couch, to impress you with my material possessions."

"Wow, you said couch and I went to a really happy place."

MAGGIE STARED at the ticket in her hand, as if she hadn't read it a hundred times. *Fifty-two.* The line had been stuck at forty-nine for the last twenty-five minutes. Rectangular fluorescent lights lined the ceiling and shone dully on the roughly two hundred occupied blue chairs filling the center of the long yellow room. The Las Vegas Department of Motor Vehicles was living up to its notoriety.

She forced her leg to stop shaking by pressing it down with her hand. Her third trip to the DMV that week was going relatively well, mostly because she'd been waiting since they'd opened at eight. That had been three hours ago. She should have brought a sandwich. *Keep calm and get your Nevada driver's license.*

Living with Chase for the last couple of weeks, she'd slowly acclimated to the idea that she would be there long enough to register it as her address. Chase, shockingly, had talked like they were now a settled couple. She grinned then covered her mouth with her hand to hide it. He was a physical man—and surprisingly affectionate. A cuddler.

Her phone beeped again with another text. There had been eight messages from Princess and four missed calls in the last hour. Princess wanted to see her, Princess wanted help, Princess was angry with Maggie for ignoring her. *I'm sorry,* Maggie had written back to the first flurry of texts, *you creeped me out. I'm not available.*

Princess hadn't given up. She'd claimed the spiking was an accident, and that she'd thought Maggie had wanted everything. It had been Maggie's fault. Then she'd gone with everyone hated her and she was going to kill herself. Maggie texted back a list of resources for her, starting with to call 211, the national crisis number for mental health and social services. Princess's last messages had a different tone.

PRINCESS

Maggie please, can I come hang out and watch tv or something? My husband, that I'm trying to divorce, found me at the brothel and caused a big scene. He broke some shit. I had to leave right away before he got out of jail. I'm totally out of money. Where do you live?

Please, Maggie. You owe me after I bought you all that stuff.

I need to chill for a while and clear my head. Find somewhere cheap to stay. I can't work until the fucking restraining order comes through.

Maggie closed her phone. The ticket counter flipped forward by one. She leaned forward and put her head in her hands. Why did she attract so many problems?

> I'll meet you at the Waffle Center on Aliante Parkway in a couple hours.

Her ticket number formed on the screen. She carried her folder of papers up to the counter, nerves churning in her stomach.

The bored-looking woman behind the plexiglass partition pulled out her documents one by one, asking Maggie to repeat what everything was three times. Was that a security thing? They needed three forms of proof of identity and two documents showing that she was living in the state of Nevada. Yesterday she'd had to drag Chase to the post office to buy a notarized statement saying that she lived at his place. The day before that she'd gone to a local office of her insurance company. She'd had to beg them to print out her papers in the office instead of sending her a packet in the mail "in one to three weeks."

"Okay, this is acceptable," said the angel behind the counter. Maggie sagged onto her elbows. "However..." Maggie stood back up, her gut clenching. "You can choose now to register to vote."

Maggie blinked. "Yes. Of course."

After getting her picture taken and being issued temporary documents, Maggie stepped outside into the perfect January weather, a comfortable sixty-five degrees. She flung out her arms and twirled in a circle. Someone coughed. One year from today, she would be eligible for in-state tuition.

Toto squeaked happily inside the mini, watching her through the window. Even with the windows down, it was getting too hot for him to spend much time inside a car. She opened her creaky door and let him outside. "You're going to have to go to doggie daycare, my friend." She petted his scruffy head. He licked her hand.

When they were back in the mini, she entered the address of the Waffle Center into her driving app. Princess was waiting for her, wacked-out and supposedly broke. Maggie had to be tough.

She wasn't going to give Princess a single cent. But she'd probably buy her a waffle. *Who do you think you're fooling?* An idea fidgeted around in her head. Once she'd had the thought, she couldn't stop turning over the possibilities and starting to make plans. It was the only thing she could really offer. The question was, why was she even considering it?

"Hey, Chase," Maggie said into her phone. She turned the ignition key, saying a little prayer of thanks when it gurgled to life. "I can't go to lunch with you. Urgent SOS from Princess—I'm meeting her to help her think through her options."

Ominous silence on the other end. She cleared her throat, forcing herself not to start babbling.

"Maggie," he said, "that's the bitch that drugged you, stole your phone, and then tried to pimp you out to some assholes. Why the hell haven't you blocked her number?"

Maggie bit her lip. It sounded pretty bad when you lined it all up like that. "She's like that horrible relative you never wanted but then are stuck rescuing for the rest of your life. If her ex-husband hadn't scared the crap out of her, we wouldn't be in touch."

"She doesn't come anywhere near my house. Hear me, woman?"

Wow, he went there pretty dang fast. "Ultimatums already?"

"Maggie, toughen the fuck up. Get that horrible human being out of your life. You can't let every exploitive predator out there have a piece of you."

"Okay, you know what, I'm done with this conversation. Who the heck do you think you are to chew me out?" she flipped her phone shut and gripped the steering wheel.

That man went from lukewarm to burning faster than alcohol on a gas flame. Life with Chase was interesting, and sometimes seared holes in the lining of her stomach. She closed her eyes and blew out a breath. The reality was she couldn't live with herself if she didn't at least meet with Princess.

CHAPTER THIRTEEN

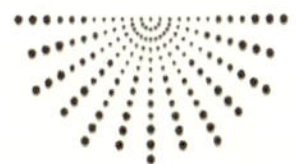

Maggie drove to the Waffle Center. It was in what Chase referred to as a shopping plaza, contractor speak for the prettier version of a strip mall. She parked in front of the tall stone building with a modern beige awning over wide glass doors.

He was working on a new shopping plaza out by Frenchman's Mountain. How the heck was she going to handle him tonight? He liked fighting. *I don't.*

The inside of the restaurant was a letdown compared to its fancy new exterior. Bare walls were painted a yellow orange, plastic cutlery and paper plates littered the tables, and old frier oil and burnt bacon were heavy in the air. Not the kind of restaurant she'd open if given the chance, but she appreciated a place with decent food that still had an option under five dollars—even if it was just flour and sugar.

She put in an order. She'd spotted Princess right away, wearing big sunglasses, hunched over at the table farthest from the door. Her hair was limp and her clothing rumpled. It hurt Maggie's heart to see her this way. The face that turned toward her was streaked with faint smears of mascara, dark bags the shade of plums under her eyes.

"Good grief, Princess, I barely recognized you."

Princess stood up and threw her arms around her, burying her face into her shoulder like a child. "Oh, my gawd, I thought you were never going to come."

She gently pushed her away and got them both into chairs at the small table. An empty cup of coffee sat in front of Princess, along with a pile of bunched-up napkins. "When can we go to your house?" Princess slouched in her chair. "I hate this little shithole. The bathroom is disgusting."

Maggie gave her a level look. Time for hard truths. "I'm staying with my boyfriend, and he's disgusted with me for even meeting you. He's still angry about you drugging me and not letting me leave. He'd probably call the police on you if you stepped on his property. I'm not kidding, Princess, it's not an option."

Princess whimpered and put her hands over her eyes. "My head aches. I think I'm getting a migraine."

"I'll split my lunch with you," Maggie said. "Food will help."

With coaxing, Princess swallowed a few bites of waffle. "It's not fair. Joshua ruined everything for me and now you're being mean about something that was an accident."

"Can you go back to the Dirty Rabbit?"

"Not until I have a restraining order."

"Wait, didn't you say he was in jail? You can get the forms online and there are people who will help you for free—"

"I don't want to deal with all that crap." Princess covered her forehead with a hand, breathing heavily. "I hate all those people, looking down their ugly stuck-up noses at me like I'm so pathetic. Fuck that. I had no idea Joshua was so angry. But it was fucking embarrassing, so I left. Divorcing costs money and is a pain in the ass. And stupid fucking Joshua wants to make it as hard as possible. Gawd, like I'd ever go near him again."

"So, what are your options?"

Princess pursed her lips. "My mother is all about me making my marriage work and finding Jesus. She'd let me stay for a few nights anyway. In Colorado."

"What about the other girls you work with? Doesn't anyone have an apartment or something?"

"Fuck those bitches," Princess said. "They're all jealous. Just because I owe a few of them money they're like ganged up against me."

Maggie sighed. She stirred her tea. Why would anyone refer to this stuff as tea? In her mind, Chase shook his head at her, cold disgust on his face. Well, she was who she was. *Dang it.*

"Okay, I have an option for you. You're not going to love it and there are conditions. Many conditions."

Princess wiped her cheeks, looking at Maggie with wide, glistening eyes. "You can lend me some money?" she said breathlessly.

"No, I can't. In fact, if I'm going to help you, you're going to have to promise to pay me as soon as you can, with a written contract, and leave me with a deposit of your most valuable possessions. Which I'll hold for you until you're back at the Dirty Rabbit or have another job. Do you want to hear more?"

Maggie stayed at the library until they closed at eight. She'd convinced herself it was because she needed to research and study, and even left a note for Chase saying that. As she stepped out into the cool night, she couldn't lie to herself anymore. She dreaded being in the same house as her boyfriend.

She chafed her cold arms, covered in goosebumps. Her gut didn't think he would ever harm her. Yet, after hearing about Princess's shattered life, she wondered if anyone could ever know.

Lights were on all over the house as she pulled into the driveway. In a chair on the front porch sat Chase, a mug in his hand. She walked up to him with a bag of books on her shoulder, and stopped at the edge of the driveway.

"Hey," she said.

"Hey, babe." He stood up and walked forward to take the bag from her. "I was wonderin' if you were going to come home."

"You mean back to your house," she said.

"Maggie." He took her hand. "Let me talk to you for a minute." His eyes raked over her face, his bushy eyebrows pinched together. Even now, after their first serious fight since becoming a couple, she couldn't wait to walk into his arms. He smelled like his soap, and his hair was wet from a shower. His callused palm was rough, the skin almost gritty. She loved his hands.

"You ignored my calls and didn't come home." He put her hand on his heart. "When you're upset, don't shut me out. At least give me a chance to talk to you."

She took a deep breath. "Seeing that girl scared by someone she'd trusted, it shook me, you know?"

Chase pulled her into his arms, and she fell in willingly. He wrapped her up too tight and her chest compressed against his. His heart beat strongly under her ear.

"I fucked up," he said against her hair. "I shouldn't have spoken to you like that."

"Princess is going to live in my trailer for a few weeks."

He held her away from him. "Babe, she's a toxic disaster…" He swallowed, staring out at the dim street for a moment. "Well, whatever happens, we'll deal with it. You have a trailer?"

Maggie sniffed, her eyes stinging. "Yeah, I do. In a little go-nowhere town in Idaho." She fanned her face. Well, now he knew she was trailer trash. "There wasn't anything else I could do, once I saw her." Her nose swelled up with fluid. Was there a supplement she could take for crying? She hadn't leaked like this since she was a kid. Chase put his arm around her waist, and they walked inside together.

She went with him, and she wanted every inch of him against her. But he was more than she'd ever thought she could handle. An old Proverbs verse had been running through her mind all evening: *A man of wrath stirs up strife, and one given to anger causes much transgression.*

"BEN, put the level on top of the cabinet before we lift it up to the marks on the wall," Chase said, watching Maggie out of the corner of his eye. The texture sprayer's compressor whirred regularly. She was slow and methodical, goggles and a respirator covering her face, her hair tied up in a red hand-kerchief. When she lifted her arms, her little plaid shirt pulled up, giving him a view of her snug-fitting jeans. He tore his glance away from her with an effort.

"Ready, boss," Ben said, sleepy patience on his face.

They lifted the new kitchen cabinet into place. When it was level, Chase cocked his arm around and drilled in a bolt with his cordless screwdriver. This little Tulle Springs home he'd bought at auction a couple of months ago was modest but in a nice neighborhood. He'd demoed it that day he'd met Maggie, a couple weeks before Christmas. After this Sunday work session with Ben and Maggie, it would be nearly ready for sale.

Ben moved carefully down his stepladder and grabbed more hardware to hand up. The kid was doing better. A touch dopey but functioning fine. He'd explained to Chase that his doctor had put him on a medication that made him sleepy and a little slow. Chase appreciated the honesty. Giving a power tool to anyone who wasn't a hundred percent there was asking for blood and missing fingertips—or much worse. Ben made up for his limitation with extra muscle. Short and stocky, with a wrestler's strength, Ben had hauled in the compressors like they were sacks of groceries.

An hour later the new white cabinet boxes were up, ready for the engineered stone counter tops. Maggie was on the back patio mixing more texture spray for the bedrooms. Toto was trying out doggie daycare—if he could get rid of Ben, there wouldn't be a thing holding them back.

"Ben, run out and grab us all hot pizza for dinner." Chase pulled out his wallet. "Maggie likes fresh tomato. I want pepperoni and olives. Get whatever the hell for yourself, soda, and a pile of napkins."

"Got it, boss." Ben pocketed the cash. Hopefully, he'd get stuck in traffic.

Chase grabbed the bottle of liquid soap he kept in his truck and headed to the backyard. His phone rang. He ignored it and the call went to voice mail after three rings.

Outside, Maggie held up an empty bucket of drywall joint compound to the light. She scratched off a white smear from the area she was reading.

"Hey, hon," she said. She'd started calling him hon a few days before. She'd said his name was too much trouble. She said hon and it was like warm honey dripped on his tongue. The damn phone in his pocket rang again. He grabbed it and saw Lucas was the caller, again. It went to voice mail.

"There are like twenty other textures we could create besides boring old orange peel," Maggie said. "Like brush the surface with a broom so the wall looks like it's covered with grass cloth wallpaper. Or notch a window squeegee to create vertical beading. Use a hair comb to make curves—and that's before we get to all the fine surface stuff like sponging and ragging and tissue paper. The decorating possibilities are endless."

Chase washed his hands with the garden hose. "Fussy detail work takes too long," he said. "But we could do something like that in the big bedroom of The Pool House. It's spacious enough to handle busy walls. Come over here and wash your hands."

"Yes." Her eyes lit up. "Carry the cabana-in-a-sunset theme inside the house in subtle ways." He held the garden hose for her while she scrubbed her hands and forearms with soap, giving him a lovely view of cleavage as she leaned over. "Where's Ben?"

"Buying dinner and hopefully taking his time about it."

Maggie glanced up at him through her lashes. "Getting a little hot under the collar? Should I spray you down with the garden hose?"

"Maybe when I'm smeared with sticky Maggie juices, I'll rinse off my face." He turned the water off and moved toward her. She backed away, a breathless huff escaping as her back hit the wall.

"Chase. This is a construction zone—what if we get tetanus in our yin yangs? Or Ben walks in? Ooof."

He braced her body with his, leaning over for a ravenous kiss. She was sweet and soft—he might never get enough. Hell, he was seriously addicted. He grabbed the waistband of her jeans, sliding his fingers onto the smooth skin under her belly button. When she wrapped her arms around his neck, he picked up her hips, forcing her to straddle him and hang on.

"Chase, I weigh a ton."

He didn't care and hardly felt it, his hands on the round curves of her ass as he carried her into the small back bedroom. It was one of the only areas of the house that hadn't been messed with much, just the old carpet and sub floor torn out and new plywood put down. He'd thrown a clean canvas tarp on the floor on his way to the backyard.

Maggie huffed. "This is totally premeditated. Do you keep condoms in your toolbox as well?"

"No, but I put them in my pocket whenever I have you around for more than five minutes." He put her on the tarp and lay on top of her, pressing his mouth onto hers. Then he moved down, kissing her neck and chest while fumbling to unbutton her shirt. Her hips pressed against him.

"We have to be fast," she said.

"Ben wouldn't remember. Too drugged up on antidepressants." His personal cell rang. She snagged it out of his pocket.

"Chase? The caller ID says Lucas."

He groaned, pressing his face against her stomach.

She answered his phone. "Hey—" Maggie's breath caught, and not in the good way he'd been working on. "Oh no, I'm so sorry to hear that. Hold on a minute and I'll grab him."

Chase rolled off her. *That asshole shithead.* His hard-on twitched in frustration. He grabbed the phone. "What?"

"Cuz, my ass is grassed. Gotta get my mom to the hospital —but I fucked up and hit a house with my friend's car. I'm in jail. Dude, I'm so glad you answered your phone."

CHAPTER FOURTEEN

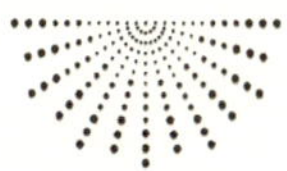

Maggie put her hands in her pockets, standing next to the wall, watching Chase wind up into one of his rages. She stayed where she was, her shoulders tight. His nostrils flared on his red face. He looked like he was about to rip his shirt off and start smashing things.

Chase put the phone in his pocket, a vein pulsing under his eye. "Lucas is in jail. My aunt needs to go to the hospital—pneumonia and a fall."

"Oh no, Chase—"

"I'm going to go over there and smack him. After I spend all night in the ER." He paced away, tight fists rubbing at his scalp. "Time to pack up our shit. I'll call Ben."

Maggie jumped into motion, stopping herself from asking him any questions. She didn't understand why he was thermonuclear because his cousin had screwed up. He had totally withdrawn into himself, like she wasn't even there.

Ten minutes later, she sat silent in the big moving-truck Chase used for his construction business. Chase drove, his hands clenched on the steering wheel. Riding in the truck with him was like being stuck in a storm cloud.

He pulled into the driveway, hit a button on the remote clipped to his fan vent and the large left bay garage door rose up as he turned off the engine.

"I'll run in and grab my book bag while you change cars." Her voice was a little hoarse from not speaking.

"You're not going with me," Chase growled. "Stay here, and lock all the damn doors. You're not in fucking Idaho. I'll be at the hospital half the night."

She swallowed against the lump in her throat. He didn't want her with him—didn't want to introduce her to his aunt. She jumped out of the truck and went into the house, not looking back.

CHASE WALKED BACK into the hospital reception area holding his full coffee cup out as he pushed open the swinging door. Selfishly, he wished Maggie was with him so that he could hold on to her. *Fucking hospitals.*

He plopped down in his chair. The coffee disappeared fast. A dull alarm buzzed in his head—she was upset with him again. Inside, he had been a raging hurricane and he hadn't wanted to touch her because he was afraid of the poison leaking out. He tossed his empty cup in the trash.

The rage had taken him by surprise. Two weeks of Maggie, and sex, and he'd almost forgotten what a screwed-up head case he was. Then she'd seemed nervous, reluctant to touch him, and he'd nearly lost it again. He rubbed his face with his free hand.

At last, a nurse led him to where his Aunt Peggy had finally gotten a room and been admitted. "She'll be here for at least a couple days," said the nurse, "with the pneumonia and wrist sprain." She glanced down at her clipboard as she held open the door for him. "She wants to see you then she needs to rest."

He stepped inside the small room, careful not to knock into any of the machines beeping around his aunt. She looked frail, the skin on her face papery and blue tinged. His heart clenched. He shouldn't have shut her out during his time in Vegas. Her eyes fluttered open. "Hey, Aunt Peggy," he said, taking her hand. "You look a lot more comfortable in that bed. I'm glad."

"Chase, thank you. When I'm better I want to meet Maggie."

He smiled. "We'll do that. Now rest. I know you're worried about Lucas but I'll bail him out tonight. I'll call tomorrow with an update."

She squeezed his fingers. "You look better. Makes me happy to see you like this."

Two hours later, after bailing out Lucas, he finally crawled into bed beside Maggie. He was careful not to wake her. She lay curled up on her side, thick hair strewn over the pillowcase. He touched the curling strands, letting them wrap around his fingers.

MAGGIE LAY in a strange dream kitchen, where heat waves from a hot oven lapped at her back and bread snuggled low against her belly. *Why am I so turned on?* A texture sprayer spewed white globs all over a three-tier cake on the counter. Overcooked, she thought, as the kitchen became covered with sticky white globules.

She swallowed, smacking her lips, her mouth and throat dry. Chase's hand on her middle came into focus, rubbing under her T-shirt. His hard body spooned around her back, his erection an enticing nudge behind her. Without a thought, she leaned her head back, cracking her eyes open enough to see his stubbly cheek.

"Good morning," he said, kissing her head. "I didn't want to leave without talking first…" He trailed off as she turned around to nuzzle into his neck, her knee rising against his leg. She was painfully ready for him, her body tight and aching.

He groaned, fumbling with a condom while she rubbed against him and kissed his neck. It took her like this sometimes in the morning—there wasn't any yesterday or tomorrow, just a humming need for him right now. While her mind was still half asleep, her body took control. Then he rolled on top of her and lunged inside. The pleasure rolled her eyes back as her body arched off the bed. They moved against each other, hard and demanding, a brisk pace as every move shook her with throbs of tingling heat. When she cried out, he pumped against her a few more times until his body spasmed with his release.

He leaned forward on his forearms, resting his forehead against hers. "God, Maggie," he whispered, "I need you so much."

She blinked, resisting falling back asleep. "What time is it?" He rolled sideways. She sat up. "How's your aunt? Is Lucas okay? I fell asleep last night earlier than I thought I would."

"Aunt Peggy has a room at the hospital. She's better." Chase scraped a hand over his face. "Lucas is out of jail and sleeping off his hangover." He kissed her shoulder. "It's a little late—will you make coffee while I shower?"

"On it." Her mind finally came online. Having sex with him first thing this morning had not, definitely not, been part of her plan last night. She'd thought herself in circles. Surely it would all start to seem worse later today. At the moment, watching his well-defined naked back, she felt a little smug that his body had slept next to hers. They were doomed as a couple, but had plenty of steam physically. *For now.*

She sighed and pulled her robe on. He'd said he needed her so much. That was new. Yeah, he needed her for sex, or at least wanted her more than the current alternatives. It was a far cry from love. She didn't know what to think about him anymore.

She had to focus on her own life and get a job in a professional kitchen. Last night she'd decided to take a step back. That was after a lot of circular thinking about how he'd never really value her. She'd paced around the empty house, which was surprisingly creepy when she and Toto were the only ones in it at night. When she'd gone out to look at her minivan, thinking seriously about spending the night at a campground, she'd realized she couldn't do that to him—not the same night he was at the hospital.

The coffee maker in the kitchen gurgled to life as she turned on the lights and started pulling food out of the fridge. The sun rising outside created a dim glow on the underside of the palm trees. With the quickness of two weeks of repetition, she had eggs cracked in a hot pan of sizzling butter before Chase had turned off the shower. And he didn't dawdle. She warmed up the English muffins and pre-cooked sausage patties in the toaster oven. Then she laid out squares of tinfoil on the counter, assembled and wrapped up his breakfast sandwiches for the road. His two-sided food cooler was clean and ready—one side for hot and the other for cold, already stocked with sandwiches and chips. On the counter she placed cookies and fruit on a plate next to a hot cup of coffee, a glass of orange juice, and a glass of water.

She dashed into the bathroom while he got dressed, avoiding eye contact as they passed. The three other bathrooms in the house were all under construction.

Despite all her doubts, she was comforted by the routine. He did need her, in small ways. Being a half of two parts was a heck of a lot less lonely than considering awkward first dates with strangers she'd met on the internet. Instead, she had her man. She huffed. He was not, by any stretch of the imagination, hers, despite him reluctantly becoming her boyfriend. He didn't want her with him when his family was involved.

With her teeth brushed, she stood up straight, a tiny bit more ready to deal with him. His face was haggard. He'd probably only gotten a few hours of sleep. She bustled into the kitchen, pouring sugar into his coffee canteen while his back was turned. He'd never complained when she thought he needed the sugar but if she asked him, he always refused. Well, he was going to need extra food too for the day he had ahead of him. She watched him shove things in his pockets, a distracted look on his face.

"Meet me for lunch at Symphony Park?" he asked.

She hesitated, glancing away from him. "Well, it's just that I know you're tired and I hate to think about you driving all that way to meet up with me."

"You're worth it." He came up to her and took her hands. Her eyebrows went up. He smelled like soap and that woodsy deodorant he put on in the morning. "I'm sorry about yesterday. I'm still…recovering from some problems I have." He pulled her against him, nuzzling her face. "Yesterday I didn't want you stuck in some waiting-room chair all night. I missed you though, babe."

He hugged her again, lifting her feet off the floor. Then he scrambled out the door, double-checking he had his phone in his pocket and his keys in his hand. She exhaled, her heart galloping in her chest.

CHAPTER FIFTEEN

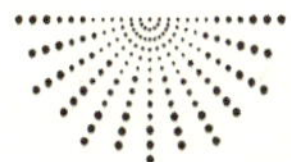

Her morning flew by in the typical Monday whirlwind of emailing and phone calls to vendors, suppliers, late payers, and subcontractors, organizing everyone into delivering what Chase needed. Her own phone sat unused next to her. Chase's calls were mostly forwarded to her, to the fancy cell phone she'd set up to use for his business.

She had an office chair now. A week ago, they'd walked into a furniture store and he'd told her to pick out a couch. She'd protested but he'd threatened to buy the first thing that he saw, which happened to be a six-thousand-dollar leather sectional set up by the front entrance. "Is that what you want?" She'd gasped. Hell no, he'd said, too heavy to lug around when he redid the family room. So they'd settled on a comfy deep sofa, designed for big people like Chase, with fabric that Maggie liked. He'd found a beautifully made all-wood coffee table, not even sniffing at the price tag.

Then he'd wanted barstools, so they'd found a couple of those. He'd ordered her to pick more stuff and finally badgered her into admitting they could use an office chair, with wheels. After the shopping trip, the family room and kitchen resembled a lived-in space.

Chase was a grab-bag of surprises. If only his rage fireworks didn't occasionally make her wonder if she was going to get her hand blown off by one of his explosions. She tapped her fingers on the table. He wouldn't physically lash out, she didn't think.

She spun in the cushy office chair. The little red light on her personal phone indicating missed calls or texts had been flashing at her for a while. They were all from Andy—she'd checked without reading them.

Since she'd moved in with Chase, she'd tapered off her texting with Andy. The truth was, she didn't want to try to explain the twists and turns her life had been taking lately— or the risks. Also, she still didn't know what to do about him insisting they should be together. The idea of losing him hurt. He'd been making some noise about moving to Vegas and hoping that they could be roommates. She'd told him no and had to state again, painfully, that their friendship had changed. After that, there had been a week of radio silence. Until this morning.

She stood up and stretched, deciding to pack for lunch with Chase before she checked her phone. She pulled a roasted chicken out of the oven, then filled a couple of slit warmed baguettes with the meat, brie, fresh tomato and pesto. Nuts, sharp cheddar cheese, and green grapes went into a Tupperware. And finally, the roasted butternut squash, cut into cubes, fresh basil, and feta salad were packed along with all the cutlery, napkins and drinks they needed for a picnic. She smiled, looking down at the pretty food. *I really might be a chef...*

She took Toto for a quick walk, then set him up with his lunch in the kitchen. After that, she had no more excuses. Tucked into a corner of the soft couch, she faced her phone.

ANDY

Maggie! There's a little Nissan parked in front of your trailer—is that you? Where's the minivan?

I'm going over there to check it out.

What the fuck. Some blonde who calls herself PRINCESS just answered your door and said she was renting it from you. You should have told me!

She's a creep. I mean she was like all over me. WTF?

I'm having a smoke but she wants me to go in there and 'party.' Ordered me to go buy beer. Fuck, Maggie, what the hell is this? Are you sure you want this girl here?

A little later:

ANDY

Holy shit. So she told me she's a sex worker. That she's legal to pay to sleep with. I said prostitution was illegal in Idaho. She said whatever and fucking went for my belt. I left. WTF?

Oh yeah and I guess you're living with some hard-ass old man now? What's the story with that?

Maggie put her head on the arm of the sofa and groaned. Princess in her hometown was going to be a disaster.

MAGGIE HIKED to the center of Symphony Park with Toto on his leash. She was headed toward a huge and bright piece of public art that appeared to be straws at different heights, all of the massive tubes a color of the rainbow. The tallest blue and purple straws were about thirty feet high, pointing straight up into the air. She walked closer until she was in its shade. She set her blanket on the decorative concrete ground. A gust of wind made the straws whistle different notes. *Oh, they're pipes.*

She leaned back on her hands. The mild warmth and blue sky felt like cheating in January. The walkways of the park were lined with palm trees above the vibrantly green fake grass. Those palm trees always gave her a zing. She definitely was not in Idaho.

"Hey, gorgeous." Chase dropped down beside her, then leaned in for a kiss. He patted Toto affectionately. His mood changes were giving her vertigo. Like the hulk explosion of yesterday had never happened, playful Chase was back.

He put his head in her lap. "Wake me up in an hour." He nuzzled her thigh.

"Food first," she said. "Especially after I lugged this heavy basket all the way from Timbuktu, where I parked."

Chase sighed but pushed himself up onto an elbow and helped her unpack the food. "What do you think of *Fanfare for the Common Man?*"

"Is that this line of pipes behind us? I like it. Reminds me of pixie sticks. When I was a kid, I hid my stash in my closet all lined up. What is it, I mean is there a story about what inspired it?"

"It's based on a piece of music. The notes turned into that." Chase flicked his thumb at the sculpture.

They ate lunch, supported against each other's shoulders, watching a couple of school buses load up with children. Leaving the children's museum, Chase said. He chatted a bit about the Symphony Park project, that it had been built on an old Union Pacific railyard, called a brownfield because of all the pollution that had accumulated there. It had been awarded gold certification for land recycling. She'd never thought about land being recycled. The park had taken them twelve years, but the city managed to get something done that would be there for a long time. It was refreshing to be away from the clutter and sunbleached grayness of Vegas. There wasn't even the distant ding of a slot machine.

"Why did you stay in Vegas?" Maggie asked.

"The numbers were right, at the time, for starting up a business. Somethin' about this place fit with me. Nice to have a little family out here too."

"Doesn't seem like you spend much time with them."

"I'm closer with my brothers and parents."

"Oh."

He hadn't spoken much about his family at all really. He sighed. "Lucas started college last year. Now he's got a Peter-Pan complex and I didn't want him thinking I was his party wingman, or his second daddy." He clenched his jaw. "He's nearly killed himself with alcohol a few times. Makes me batshit crazy."

She took his hand. She wished she had a cousin. "Well, he's lucky to have you."

He looked drawn, his eyes blinking. "I'm going to talk to him. Check up on him more, try to force that cheese puff to grow up and be a decent man."

"Cheese puff?" She huffed. "You know the last time he was over I think he carried a bag of those around."

"It killed me last night, thinking of him driving drunk and having an accident. That the last thing I said to him was 'get the fuck out before I shove your shoulder up your ass.' Damn moron."

"Yeah, he screwed up."

"My aunt's been sick for a while. She's on her own with

Lucas—his father left for Florida and remarried years ago. They don't see him."

"I'm sorry to hear that."

They were quiet for a while, while the musical pipes behind them made soft toots and whistles. Hearing about his family problems reminded her how alone she'd become. Gran had cut ties with her extended family for various reasons, and they were far away in any case. Grandpa Billy had been an only child raised by grandparents, like her. And here she was considering walking away from a man who seemed to care about her.

She rested back on her hands. "Why were you so angry yesterday, before you went to the hospital?" There, she'd said it. She closed her eyes, realized she was holding her breath and exhaled. She needed to know.

"Hey," he said, drawing a circle on her knee. "I'm sorry about that. I'll work on it, I promise."

"Okay." She didn't know what else to say. His volatility seemed like a part of him.

"I lost two close friends in Afghanistan." His voice was flat. She opened her eyes and saw his Adam's apple bobbing.

"I'm so sorry," she said, lamely, reaching out to touch his hunched-in shoulder.

He stood up and took a drink from his water bottle, facing away from her. "Talking about it stirs it up." He lay back down.

She ran her fingers through his hair and resisted the urge to start asking questions and lead him along. Maybe it wasn't the right time for him to talk about it. Her gut was telling her to wait, so she did. But what did she know? He needed to talk to a therapist.

"First was a guy in my platoon. He was the one who got everyone laughing even when we were stuck inside the back of a truck going over bad road for six hours. Marcus. It was my job to keep him safe, and I didn't. I should have been fucked in that land-mine explosion, but I walked away, a little scratched up. Wasn't right."

Maggie took his hand. He gripped hers so tight the bones in her hand knocked together. After a moment, he relaxed, breathing heavily next to her.

"The other was my best friend who I'd convinced to join up with me. His squad got hit hard by gunfire and he was shot several times. I watched his casket loaded up into a C-130, then flown out of that fucking desert."

The silence lengthened. How did anyone emotionally survive war? "You blame yourself," she said.

He turned to look at her. "I became a rage maniac trying to keep everyone safe while I finished out my service. But when I came back to civilian life I couldn't switch back. I've told you a bit about the ranch, my parents, and brothers. Being out there helped, for a while, but I was restless—and too angry, even there. Then I came out here and got messed up again." He rubbed his face. "When we met, that was my worst. Lately, I've thought I'd turned a corner. Then Lucas screwing up flipped a switch inside me." He stared up, his eyes distant and a little lost.

She bent over him, moving in close, cupping his face with her hands. "It's not your fault," she said, a little sharper than she'd meant to. She took a deep breath. "You did the best you could." He kissed her palm.

"I know I upset you yesterday," he said pressing her palm against his cheek to keep it there. "I'm going to work on it."

She didn't know what to think.

CHAPTER SIXTEEN

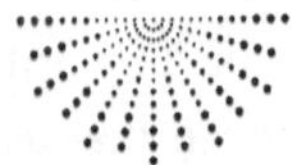

At the end of the next week, early Saturday morning, Maggie did a double take as her eyes scanned over Chase's email. *ARE YOU KEEPING MY SON FROM ME?* was written in one of the subject lines, shouting at her in capital letters. She stared at the bright white and blue inbox screen.

The office chair clicked as she pushed back into it. Chase's mother had sent the email to his work account. Air puffed out of her chest. She leaned forward, put her cursor over SON and double clicked.

To the TRAMP occupying Chase's house,

This is Chase's mother, Dolly. Already I have serious doubts about your relationship with my son. He needs a strong woman that is close to his family. If you care about him, you'll do the right thing and not hold him back from the life he'll eventually go to. An important girlfriend is ready to reconnect with him. They were extremely close, both from similar backgrounds, with families used to meeting in the same social circles.

Lucas has told me a bit about you and it's clear you're also holding yourself back by the abnormal work connection you have with my son. Take some advice, given with honest sincerity, that the physical attraction between two people never lasts. What do you think you can offer him other than your body? It sounds to me like nothing.

I travel in influential circles, am friends with people that affect Chase's business. There is much I could do to limit his ability to prosper. The fact that he has not even introduced you to me tells me that he knows I would disapprove of your murky background. I think he is ashamed of you. If you insist on clinging on to him, you'll force my hand.

These communications are for your eyes only. I'm prepared to contact every chef in the city to keep you from working. Poison my son against me and there will be consequences for your career. I'll expect to hear from you in the next twenty-four hours. Dolly.

Maggie blinked over her wide-open eyes. *What the heck?* That email had had her glued to the screen like the climax of a horror film. She stood up. Then leaned over and turned off the screen. Tripping on the office chair, she backed away from the computer like it was a coiled snake. Toto barked.

He's ashamed of you, you offer him nothing, ran through her head on repeat. His old girlfriend wanted to get back together with him? Another one besides the stalker?

She pulled her hair into a tight ponytail with shaky hands as she paced around the kitchen. Toto watched her with his head cocked. She'd been living with Chase for almost a month now—and not focusing enough on her own goals.

Most of the reason she'd stuck it out with her ex-boyfriend, Todd, for five years was because of his family. His mother had called her on the phone to chat, remembered her birthdays, pulled her in for hugs. She'd crammed in on the rough-around-the-edges sofas in the family room every football Sunday and loved it. The worst part of breaking up with Todd was losing his family. It was what she'd wanted all her life.

The cold kitchen countertop cooled her hot cheeks as she pressed her face against it. She tapped her fingers on the smooth surface. There was a hive in her head, buzzing and stinging. She wanted to throw herself into a three-day cooking project. But she couldn't move, stiff with poison from that email.

"La la la," she whispered. She needed an army of Munchkins singing, and a pair of ruby slippers to take her home. There was a wicked witch out to get her.

CHASE DIALED MAGGIE AGAIN, tapping as he waited for her to pick up. He gripped the steering wheel. Something had happened. She usually took ten minutes tops to return his calls and he'd been trying to reach her for two hours.

"Call me," he said tersely into her voice mail and hung up.

Camilla waited to meet him at the coffee shop inside her white Cadillac XT5, a phone to her ear. He sighed and jumped out of his truck. Heels emerged from her SUV door first, a diamond anklet sparkling. Her lean figure was dressed, as usual, in designer clothing fit for a corporate board meeting. Her long dark hair was perfectly in place. He nodded at her, putting his hand in his pockets. She flashed a toothy white smile, immediately coming in for a perfume-clouded hug.

He managed to stop himself glancing at his watch. They were next door to his job site, but his day had gone sideways. There wasn't a good reason to be rude, even though she'd obviously lied about desperately needing his help and advice on a business matter. The truth was, he had his own agenda.

He held the door open to the chain coffee shop. She sashayed in ahead of him, gazing over her shoulder at him like they were going into a club to dance.

She stepped up to the counter and said, "I'll have an iced grande skinny soy vanilla latte, decaf, no foam, sugar-free, extra shot, double blended, two pumps of vanilla syrup, caramel sauce, extra drizzle." The seventeen-year-old behind the counter wrote notes and nodded with slumped shoulders. "Thanks."

Chase paid for both of their drinks, because Camilla had walked away, while checking his phone again for a message from Maggie. Nothing.

She picked a loveseat in the corner of the cafe and then was obviously disappointed when he pulled up a chair.

"So, what's the problem, Camilla?" He took a drink of his black coffee.

"Oh, hang on. It's so warm in here." She wiggled out of her tight tailored jacket, flashing her cleavage at him. Her forehead was broken up by heavy dark eyebrows that always appeared quirked, the edges raised in a question. He'd been a little in love with her, a long time ago. Now, he could admire her loveliness and also be relieved things hadn't worked out. Looking back, he'd been more in love with the idea of her, with the life he'd thought they'd have together. Who she actually was as a person hadn't been foremost in his mind.

"Well," she said, taking a deep breath. "The board wants to tear down those cheap apartments Daddy put up, oh, I can't remember when exactly but they look very nineties. Anyway, now they want to put a new development in and sell it all off. What do you think?"

Chase rattled off a list of concerns for her to think about —mostly to follow the letter of the law when evicting all the low-income tenants and, hopefully, have some compassion. With housing making money again in Vegas, everyone with the means was redeveloping as fast as they could find the labor. He'd go through a formal bid process with the board, before he'd be willing to work for them.

"How are you?" she said, changing the subject. "I've been hoping to see you for ages."

"Keeping busy," he said. The diamond-studded cross twinkled against her neck. If he hadn't met Maggie, maybe something would have happened. He was a different person than the young ambitious man he'd been before going to war. She seemed the same. Camilla was conventional, she wanted a big house in the suburbs, kids, and a pure-bred dog. She golfed, he remembered, and used to drag him out on the green every weekend. She'd forced him to wear a polo shirt.

"I'm divorced now, Chase," she said, her face drawn and serious. "The worst mistake of my life is finally over." She glanced at him meaningfully.

"It wasn't a mistake," he said. "Your daughter is lovely."

She smiled. "Sophie is wonderful. You're going to love her." Chase frowned. Hell, he wished Maggie was here. Camilla was going to force him to say it. She reached over and put her hand on his. "I could care for you very well. Remember those long days we used to spend in bed? I think about them, about you, often."

He turned his hand over under hers. "Sweetheart," he said, "that was a long time ago."

~

CHASE SAT down on the floor and pulled off his dirt-covered boots. He needed to brush them off. His back landed against the wall and he closed his eyes. Maggie's clunker minivan was gone. And he was too damned tired to run after her.

Working so many hours that you didn't have time to think was all well and good when you were a lonely miserable bachelor. If he hadn't put in twelve hours on a Saturday, he would have been around to pin Maggie down before she ran off—and he could have talked some sense into her.

His legs ached. They were going to cuddle in front of a movie tonight, her choice. He'd planned to distract her with hot sex. And to exchange foot rubs again. Then he'd fall asleep while she finished her movie until it was time to go to bed. And have sex again.

Instead, he had to get off the floor and go chase down his girl. He wasn't sure he wanted to. Let her spend the night in her van at the campground. Maybe it would dawn on her that she'd made a pretty shitty choice.

They'd known this hellish Saturday was coming all week as the plaza project cranked up in intensity and it got closer to deadline. Getting all of the subcontractors to finish on time brought him back to his sergeant days and being the hard-ass that couldn't care less about your personal crisis. He'd chewed out three idiots today. Finally, the HVAC was up and running and the electrical was ready for inspection. The whole time he'd wanted to drop everything and run back to the house to check on Maggie. But that would have enabled everyone else to ditch out, the domino effects stretching into the next week.

He'd had a text from her a few hours after coffee with Camilla. *Having a horrible day,* she'd written, *got a couple nasty emails. We'll talk tomorrow, today is too busy.* And that was it. She hadn't answered his calls and hadn't responded to more texts. He was beyond frustrated with her.

His phone buzzed in his pocket. He snatched it out and deflated when he saw the screen.

"Hey," Chase said. "What's the shit show?"

"Relax," Lucas said in his dumb surfer guy voice. He chewed on something crunchy. Chase held the phone away from his ear. "I need work, man. You got anything for me?"

"Yeah," Chase said, "it won't be glamorous so leave your sparkly dress at home. But if you can muscle out some grunt work for me, I'll find somethin'."

"Donk funkulous."

"Lucas, I see you even touch alcohol and that's it, you're out for good. No drinking or drugs of any kind. And if you think I'll be all soft and cuddly because you're my cousin, you won't last an hour. I'll be harder on you. And expect those flabby arms to shake by the end of the day. You got me?"

"Yes, sergeant. Damn, you're a hard-ass."

"My ass can cut concrete."

Lucas laughed. "Tell Maggie thanks for the sweet goods. Made me want to pull out Bubbles so I could keep eating after my stomach was a bloated basketball."

"You named your bong Bubbles." Of course he did.

"Six feet of sweet-ass draw. Bubbles would mellow out your uptight ass."

Chase focused on a folded note on the kitchen counter. "Listen, I have to go—Maggie's upset about some email."

Lucas made a sympathetic grunt.

Chase cleared his throat and forced himself to say, "It makes me throw up in my mouth to say this but I'm, uh, glad you're okay. Take care, k?"

"Whoa, that was disgusting. But, uh, yeah, thanks. You too." They hung up.

Chase sniffed, embarrassed with himself.

The note, several pages torn out of a notebook, was tucked under a plate of cookies. Of course. As if a plate of peanut butter cookies was going to smooth over her disappearing out of the blue. But they did taste good. He unfolded the paper, revealing her slanted and loopy handwriting.

Chase,

Hey. There's pasta in the fridge you can either heat up or eat cold, and a salad too. Your business notes are filed. 5 bid requests today. Wow.

No doubt you're a little mad at me right now for not talking to you. I'm sorry I'm not the kind of woman that can deal with you—a better woman. I feel so out of place all of a sudden, like I'm an Eskimo shedding my furs in the desert, trying to build an igloo out of sand. Or maybe a plain scoop of vanilla offered to Ben and Jerry…where's all the good stuff, they'd say.

Well, you probably want to know why I'm not there right now. The short answer is I've rented an apartment and was able to move in right away. It's a decent complex with a fitness center and a pool and only about 500 a month. My one bedroom is a shoebox but at least I have a tiny kitchen. It was a little more than the studio I was originally thinking about but those studios don't come with an oven.

How could anyone survive without fresh baked cookies?

I want you to know I'm safe behind a locked door and not sleeping on the floor of my van. I won't let anyone in. If someone knocks there is a peep hole and also a chain. But the place seemed pretty quiet. Relax, you had a long day. I'm reading pastry books or moving things around in my tiny kitchen.

The long answer is I'm upset and need a little time to think. Your mother wrote an email to me this morning. I've deleted it because you don't need that winding you up. She made it clear that I'll never be good enough for you and that there's a wealthy ex-girlfriend waiting in the wings. And then you texted that you were meeting her for coffee—the woman your mother wants you to marry. Also, the other ex, the stalker ex, sent more naked pictures today (erased).

And to top it all off Princess is stirring up trouble back in Idaho. I knew she would, I just didn't expect it so soon or bad. Okay, yeah, I was hoping it would all be fine. Well, it's not.

I'll be there tomorrow for the usual Sunday morning cook to get food ready for your week.

I've been offered an internship with a pastry chef downtown, at Paris on the strip actually. He's a celebrity in the pastry world and regularly lets people like me into his kitchen, willing to work for free, for short periods. It will be early weekday mornings for the next week. I'll be able to do everything for you as usual except in the early mornings. We can talk about this tomorrow. You probably never imagined you'd pay me this long in the first place so I know there's a limit to how much work you can give me. Just let me know.

I'm thinking about you, and missing you.

Xo Maggie

Chase read the letter three times, the paper crinkling in his tight grip. She'd left him without even a face-to-face conversation. He picked up the plate of cookies and threw it against the wall. Shards of porcelain and brown crumbs scattered over the floor.

CHAPTER SEVENTEEN

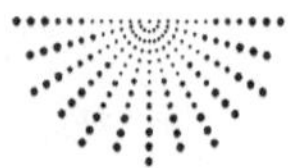

The old vinyl window snagged and creaked, resisting Maggie as she pushed it open inch by inch. Toto circled the room, sniffing the carpet with his tail wagging.

She should have known that the scented candle burning when she'd viewed the apartment had been masking a world of cat odor. At least they allowed pets. She'd handed over a pile of money, signed a stack of papers, then dashed back to Chase's to get more of her stuff and finish her work there.

"Welcome to the Sweet Palm Community," the assistant manager had said around the wad of gum in her mouth. She handed over two keys, her manicured nails careful not to touch Maggie's hand.

Laughter and thumping music vibrated the walls from down the hall. It was Saturday night and the place had started to get lively. Maggie hopped up on the narrow kitchen island that separated the main room. She could just fit her bottom and head on it when she lay down, her knees bent. Blowing her breath out in a long sigh she tried to still the whirling tornado of her thoughts.

Chase. He was home now, maybe sitting on that comfy

couch, drinking beer and watching SportsCenter for the football highlights. She had exiled herself to a cell with no furniture or television.

"The best view comes after the hardest climb," she said out loud.

"If you don't know where you're going, any road will get you there," she said to hear another one. That was a Lewis Carroll quote Grandpa Billy had told her when she'd been anxious.

He was the one she'd spent the most time with as a kid. He'd been disabled and her grandmother worked every hour she could get at the grocery store. Billy liked to chat, endlessly interested in whatever he could get her to talk about. When she'd cooked, he'd put on the radio and do his best to help. He was always happy to see her, always thrilled with whatever she made in the kitchen, disaster or minor triumph. He was the sweetest man she'd ever known.

He'd died of sudden heart failure when she was fifteen years old. She'd nearly dropped out of school. Had started drinking, then having sex, staying out late and ignoring her grandmother.

She swallowed, grief welling up. "You've got a good heart, Maggie girl," Billy used to say to her. "You're gonna make your gran proud." She'd wanted to make them both proud. A year after his death, Maggie had settled down, remembering his words, knowing how much he'd wanted her to turn out right.

She hadn't exactly been fair to Chase. Here she was lying on a kitchen counter as her phone flashed next to her with his missed calls and text messages. Grandpa Billy might say, "Chin up, girlie. Ain't nobody better than anybody else and don't you forget it." Chase's mother thought she was trash. She'd known his family was better off than hers growing up, most were, but she hadn't realized until reading that email today that it was more like they were from different planets.

She picked up her phone and texted him.

> Hey, still awake?

Seconds later her phone rang. She swallowed.

"Hi," she croaked.

"Maggie," he growled. "Where the hell are you?"

"I told you in the note—"

"No, you didn't. What apartment are you at?"

She was silent for a few long seconds. "You wouldn't like it here. I've got even less furniture than you do. I'll be there tomorrow, okay?"

"No, it's not fucking okay." He took a deep breath. She could hear him pacing around and a bottle slammed down on the counter. "How the hell would you like it if I took off 'to think,' moved out without even talking to you first?"

She sat up, rubbing her face, trying to marshal some kind of reasonable response. "I thought you'd be a little relieved. I mean, I was just there temporarily until I got my own place. It's not like we agreed to live together." Good grief, she sounded like he meant nothing to her. Didn't he know it was the opposite problem?

"Why won't you tell me where the hell you are?"

"I don't want you storming over here tonight to yell at me. Besides, I'm the only one who needs to suffer in this shoe box."

He breathed heavily into the phone.

She imagined his nostrils flaring like a dragon's. "Are you, um, in a rage?" Yeah, pointless question. He'd probably broken things. His grunt was her only answer. "Why did you meet with Camilla today?" she asked in her best impression of a businesslike voice. Because she was so freakin' mature. *Right.*

He blew out a breath. "Is that what this is about? She begged me to talk to her about a construction issue so I agreed to twenty minutes at a coffee place close to the job site. It was nothing to me, Maggie. I don't want her back in my life. We were never right for each other. I told her about you so she'd move on."

Maggie watched a car drive by on the road below her window. "Your mother thinks that's who you'll end up with," she said. "Or someone like her. She called me a tramp." She wrinkled up her nose but forced herself to go on. "I think you see me as a poor little sex worker you're helping out." She sounded so pathetic.

"I don't. You're my girlfriend. And my mother wrote you? Doesn't sound like her. What pisses me off is your damn double standard. What about you leaving me as if I'm nothing more than a pit stop on your road trip?"

She inhaled, wiping the wetness off her cheeks with her shirt. "Chase," she croaked around the lump in her throat, "I don't feel that way, you know I don't. I'm crazy about you and it scares the crap out of me."

They both breathed into the phone. Chase said, "If you hadn't gotten that email, you'd be here. You should have showed it to me."

She took a drink from her bottle of water. "She brought to the surface stuff I've been worried about for a while."

"Maggie."

"There were threats about smearing my reputation with chefs."

"It was from that fucking stalker. My mother would never write that."

She exhaled. The stalker was pretending to be his mother now? *To scare me off.*

Chase muttered to himself, seemingly caught up in a tempest. Surprisingly, she wished she was there, so that she could soothe him with her body until they fell asleep. They were both in for a bad night.

She said, "I'm sorry I worried you, and that I panicked and left. I'm going to stay here tonight though. I miss you."

He sighed, the silence stretching out as she listened to him pick up a bottle and put it down. "Fine, we'll talk tomorrow." He hung up.

CHAPTER EIGHTEEN

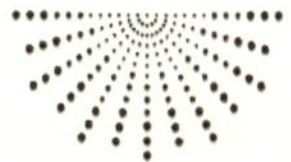

The cascading chimes of the doorbell startled Maggie into hitting her head on the dryer opening she had crouched in. Toto barked, pawing at the laundry room door. Waking up at three that morning, to get adjusted to her internship schedule, had not helped her coordination. Whoever was at the door could hold their horses—or leave. She'd rather not talk to anyone.

She pulled out the rest of the dry sheets and towels and quickly stacked them in the laundry basket so they wouldn't wrinkle up. She transferred Chase's clean wet clothes into the dryer.

She pushed up to her feet with the basket against her hip. The one person she had to talk to was Chase. Her stomach grumbled. She'd been running around all morning doing the shopping before arriving at the house tense and ready for a confrontation. Instead, his truck was gone and there had been a quiet inside, her cookie plate broken on the floor, and beer cans stacked on the counter.

The doorbell chimed again, someone holding down the

button. She huffed. That was just rude. Toto ran out of the laundry room growling and barking, and positioned himself in front of the door.

She was tempted to ignore whoever it was. It was almost lunch time and she and Chase didn't need someone here delaying the conversation they were going to have.

She hustled the sheets into the bedroom by the front door, ignoring the two blurry figures she could see through the frosted glass. It was probably another set of missionaries. There were a stunning number of young men in suits knocking on doors everywhere you looked around Vegas. Was Sin City the frontline of the battle?

When the people at the door started knocking, she threw down the pillow she was stuffing into a case and marched to the door. Whoever it was had an earful coming. She locked the now frantic Toto in the bedroom. Standing on her tiptoes, she peered through the peephole, and froze.

"Hey," came a muffled shout. "We know Maggie's in there. Open the damn door."

She put a hand over her eyes, the bottom dropping out of her stomach. Oh no. Bang bang bang. The entire weekend was turning into a nightmare. She wanted to crawl into that clean bed and ignore it all.

Putting her chin up, she forced herself to move her hands. The dead bolt scraped back as she turned it. She took a deep breath and opened the door.

In front of her stood Andy, arms crossed over his chest, black hair dangling in his eyes. And beside him was a familiar middle-height man with short blond hair and a bit of a belly under his polo shirt. He had his baseball cap on backward, as always. Her ex-boyfriend. Todd's teeth flashed between his thin beard and mustache.

"Mags." Todd stepped forward and grabbed her into a hug.

She muttered an "oof," her eyes wide. He'd always been a big hugger. He lifted her feet off the floor, pressing her chest into his as he swung her around in a circle.

"Todd," she croaked, "put me down." Her feet touched the front porch and she managed to push herself away.

"What the hell is this?" Chase stalked over from the driveway.

She took a moment to straighten her T-shirt and smooth down her shorts. "I'm not sure, Chase. These are friends of mine that I grew up with in Idaho. I had no idea they were coming." She turned toward Andy. He stood there glaring, his fingers twitching. "How did you find me, Andy? I haven't given this address to you."

"I downloaded an app." Andy flicked hair out of his eyes.

"You were at an apartment complex last night. We drove by but figured you were sleeping." Todd chuckled.

Maggie blinked. "Wait—you illegally tracked my phone?"

Chase leaned in the doorway next to her. Tension radiated off him. She kept her gaze on Andy.

"We need to talk to you, Mags," Andy said. He glared at Chase for a moment. "Alone."

"Let's grab some brunch." Todd smiled affably. "My treat."

She put a hand over her eyes. "Guys, this isn't a good time. Maybe later—"

"I've been talking to Princess," Andy said, red spreading over his face. *Oh boy.* She had a bad feeling she knew where this was going.

"Oh right, Princess," Maggie said. Cold dread crawled down her spine. "Of course."

"I know you're in trouble," Andy said. "That he coerced you and treats you badly—he dragged you out of that club you were at with Princess. That he threatened everyone you were with just for talking to you."

Maggie stared up at the sky then closed her eyes, blowing

out a breath. "Andy, that is a twisted load of crap. That night Princess drugged me then wouldn't let me leave. She freaking stole my phone. What a liar."

"If that's true then why the hell would you let her stay at your place?"

"If it was true?" Maggie pointed at their car, her arm shaking. "Get out! I've had enough of this crap."

"Whoa, baby doll." Todd held up his hands. "Just come have some lunch with us. I want to talk to you."

"No, Todd," Maggie said stiffly. "I have lunch plans."

"Sweetheart." Todd reached his hand out to her. "You don't need to sell yourself for money. I had no idea things were so tight. Let's go to Lake Tahoe—road trip."

All the blood drained out of her face. She stumbled to the side, grabbing the door to keep herself upright. Chase slipped an arm around her waist.

"I'm not," she managed to get out. "Todd, I'm not selling myself."

"Oh, yeah," Andy said, his red face tight, "are you trying to say you didn't leave home to go work in a brothel? At the Dirty Rabbit. That you didn't meet this asshole there?"

Maggie's ears were ringing. Chase said something to the other guys but she couldn't hear it. She closed her eyes as dots swam on the back of her eyelids. Then she scrambled for the edge of the open sided porch, landed on her knees painfully, and heaved onto the red lava rock landscaping.

"Get off my property," Chase said coldly. "You've upset Maggie enough with this bullshit."

She let Chase pull her to her feet and take her inside. He supported her past the wide staircase and into the bathroom.

She leaned over the faucet and rinsed out her mouth. Then she tilted further in and let the cold water run over her face. The worst thing had happened. By now everyone Andy and Todd knew in Ridgeview thought she was a prostitute working in a brothel—which was the whole small town.

She stood up and stared at herself in the mirror. Smudges of makeup pooled beneath her puffy eyes. Her nose was red on her pale drawn face. She couldn't ever go back to Ridgeview. A golf-ball-shaped lump welled in her throat.

A cool pair of hands settled on her shoulders. She couldn't move, holding on to the sink as her chest heaved and her shoulders shook. A towel dropped over her shoulder and then Chase lifted her up in his arms, cradling her against his chest with her knees draped over one of his elbows. The sudden swift movement made her catch her breath. He carried her to the couch and sat down with her on his lap. She wiped her face on the towel, not resisting when he pulled her head down onto his shoulder. He kicked off his boots and put his feet up on the couch, with a deep sigh.

"This," he said, kissing the top of her head, "is where we were supposed to be last night." He combed the hair away from her face. "Except, I would have been the one crying— over your movie choice."

She sniffed. "You don't even know what I like to watch."

"Oh, so the cartoon movie about the rat who becomes a chef was a coincidence? It gave me the creeps."

"You're full of it."

He tucked hair behind her ear. "I'm sorry that your friends did that to you."

She gulped, her eyes filling again.

"It's obvious they care about you. In their own idiotic way."

"Yeah," she said, swallowing. "That was some stupid tenderness."

She closed her eyes and focused on breathing, taking in the salty pine and cedar smell that was Chase. His hands smoothed down her back, pausing to massage the tight muscles along her spine. Her pelvis tightened with the warm yearning coming to life in her core. She wanted to roll over and put her face in his neck. Pull that T-shirt up and run her hands over his hard abs and chest. She swallowed. Chase turned his head, his lips grazing the top of her ear. Her body tensed in anticipation, ready to pull him down on top of her, wrap her legs around his waist…

"I'm going to make tea," she said in a strangled voice. His hands lingered on her as she pushed herself off the couch. "Coffee?" she called back to him.

He was staring at her with intense concentration. "What I want," he said, "is for you to come back over here and lie down with me. You'll feel a hell of a lot better if you do."

She filled the kettle. "We need to talk," she called to him, her voice trembling. Wow, heck of a time she was picking. But on the other hand, she wanted to have this entire horrible day over with. Cut all her ties and start over. Find some new life where she wasn't a sex worker and a homeless destitute woman, variously pitied and shamed by those who knew her.

Chase didn't move from the couch. She couldn't wait for the kettle to boil. Hands a little shaky, she turned off the stove. Was she doing this? She spotted her cell phone and loaded it into her pocket then slung her purse over her shoulder.

"Going somewhere?" Chase said from the living room.

She pulled the office chair over and sat across the coffee table from him. Taking a breath, she stared down at her hands. "When we met, you made it clear you weren't looking for a relationship." She closed her eyes, trying to get this right, fumbling for the words to order themselves in her scrambled brain. "You wanted to pay me for sex so that we had clear boundaries between us."

"Maggie," Chase interrupted, "I was in a bad place. I've

still got a way to go, but that's not me anymore. And it's not us."

"I'm always going to be that girl to you, Chase," she said. "The one you don't want to introduce to your family. The one your friends saw you meet at a brothel."

"Wait—you think I'm ashamed of you?"

"I'm ashamed of me. I need to start over. Get away from all these people that saw me make the worst mistake of my life."

Chase swung his feet to the floor with a bang. "What does it matter what those assholes think?"

"You don't understand." She was trying to stay calm, but her throat was raw and tight. "I grew up in a trailer, Chase. Any respect I ever earned was thrown at me like crumbs— wow, good job you poor little doomed piece of trash, we're so proud of you for finishing high school. And, oh my gosh, you can hold a job." She swallowed, pinching the webbing between her finger and thumb, focusing on the pain. "I don't want to be that girl anymore. I have to start over. Work hard enough that it won't matter where I come from."

"What the hell does that have to do with us?" Chase scratched his chin. "That shit doesn't matter to me."

"It's been pretty clear from the beginning that you see this as a temporary relationship. You finally bent enough to call me your girlfriend, but I've never deluded myself into thinking that you could have long-term feelings for me."

Chase rubbed his face. "I'm not going to lie to you—I don't know what I want. And it's like you're putting a gun to my head."

Maggie stood up. "I'm leaving. Thank you for everything you've done for me." She walked away, resisting the urge to run. Toto rushed out of the bedroom when she opened the door, and stood up against her legs as she put on his leash.

A rough hand caught her wrist. "Hey," Chase said. "This

isn't over between us. I can't force you to stay, but I'm damn tired of you running away. All that noise you're ashamed of doesn't matter, Maggie. What this is about is you being afraid." He let go of her and turned around, walking back into his house.

CHAPTER NINETEEN

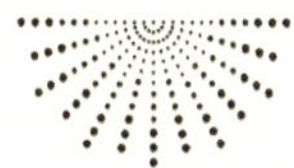

Maggie was put to work as soon as she arrived in the large commercial kitchen, with a handful of other people, at three thirty in the morning. The famous Andre, the young and attractive Brazilian who had become a minor celebrity in Vegas, was nowhere in sight.

A scowling older woman held a hairnet out. "Double-check your shedding," she commanded. The chef had her hair cropped short, bleached blonde, and spiked with gel on the top of her head.

"Yes, chef," Maggie said promptly.

She set to work on whatever the chef commanded her to do. There were hundreds of cookies to make, and sheet pan after sheet pan of filled croissants. She lost track of the number of pie crusts she prepped for the variety of quiches the kitchen put out.

The counter became covered with breads of all kinds, little tarts, muffins, and parfaits. Two hours sped by. The head chef snapped at her to break for coffee and a roll, which Maggie did gratefully. It might be her imagination, but she thought there was a grudging hint of approval in the way the chef glanced over her handiwork. She'd certainly given her a lot to do and had inspected every tray of prep work she'd done before it was passed on down the line for filling and baking.

Maggie ate fast, planning to be back at her station early. She needed to show how eager she was to be there. Her phone beeped and she saw a text from Chase. Her heart clenched. Yesterday felt like a bad dream—she'd broken up with him, she reminded herself. And quit her job. Her stomach clenched as panic welled inside her. She'd thrown herself right back in the fire.

CHASE

Hey babe, I miss you. If you thought you were quitting on me yesterday, you're wrong. This week is going to be hellishly busy. You better be here during the day to keep things going. I'll be looking forward to my dinner tonight.

Maggie scowled. *Hey babe?* The man took her as seriously as a squirrel blocking his path. She gulped back the rest of her coffee and drank a glass of water. Those dark hazel eyes of his hovered in her head, watching her with stubborn determination.

She scrubbed her hands in the sink. Her eyes were puffy and swollen in the small mirror on the wall. Last night she'd cried herself to sleep, for the whopping five hours she'd managed before getting up at two-thirty. She'd questioned her sanity—why was she walking away from that kind of man, even if it wouldn't last? Would she ever get over him? She doubted it.

He'd texted her like nothing had happened. She punched into a pile of cold dough, ignoring the questioning look of the sous-chef next to her.

~

CHASE HIT the unlock button on his key fob. The big black truck double-beeped, flashing its lights cheerfully. *Welcome back, driver. Time to travel to your empty house and emptier bed.* He pinched the bridge of his nose. If it wasn't a Monday night, he'd take himself straight to a tavern and claim a barstool until they closed.

"Hey, baby," said a low throaty voice.

His pulse jumped, his gaze snapping up to look at her face. The woman in wobbly high heels and a trench coat wasn't Maggie.

"Chase," purred his ex-girlfriend and stalker, Steph, leaning against his truck. "Let's go somewhere and talk. I have something important to tell you."

He blew out his breath. The trench coat slipped open, revealing that she wasn't wearing much underneath, only underwear and pantyhose.

He threw his bag into the back of the truck, body responding to her a little and hating himself for it. She was thinner. He glanced at her again and saw the sharp edge of her clavicle bone sticking out above her chest and the outline of her skull under the hollow of her cheeks. He sucked in a breath. Responsibility and a sick disgust for himself settled onto his shoulders.

"Steph, I told you not to follow me. We're done. I know you've been sending things to my work email. My girlfriend erased them for me. You need to stop this."

"I'll always be here for you," she said. Her pupils were dilated. He'd seen that glassy look enough to know she was on something and barely functioning. "I know what you need. I need it too. I won't ask any more of you, baby. I was out of line—give me another chance."

Ben, Jose, and Johnny walked up to his truck. Their faces

were carefully blank, but he knew they'd come over to see the show. Well, the asswipes could pay their dues for it.

"Steph, give me your keys."

She hesitated for a moment then handed them over, her face gazing up at him hopefully. He wanted to stick a screwdriver in his gut.

He pressed the key fob and there was a distant beeping a block away. "Johnny, go get Steph's car." He tossed the keys. "She's not in the best shape to drive."

"You got it, boss." Johnny jogged off down the street that was lined with construction fencing.

"Ben, can you come with us to that diner over there?" Chase pointed at the chain restaurant a few blocks away.

"Sure, no problem."

"Sorry, boss," said Jose, "I'd help with whatever but Maria's gonna kill me if I'm any later. We got engaged last weekend." He smiled.

"Congratulations." Chase clapped him on the shoulder. "That's great news." His stomach twisted, a twinge of envy for that happy look on Jose's face.

Johnny pulled up in Steph's car. Inside were a pair of jeans and a T-shirt on the passenger seat. Chase put everything he found on the floor of her car into a bag and handed it to Steph, who was sitting inside his truck. Johnny left with Jose. Ben drove the little sedan over to the diner.

Chase drove the few blocks to the restaurant, not saying a word. "Go put your clothes on in the bathroom," he told Steph. He got out of the truck to hold her door open. "Meet me at our table. Then we'll talk."

She had sat there docile and silent but at his words she moved jerkily out of the truck.

He ordered food for her, knowing she'd refuse to order if he asked her. She slid into the booth next to him and he had to fight the urge to scoot away.

"Steph, this is Ben, a friend of mine who's been dealing with some mental health issues since getting out of the army." He'd talked to Ben before Steph got out of the bathroom about what he wanted to do. Still, he watched Ben's face to make sure he was handling it okay. Ben gazed sympathetically at Steph and nodded.

"It was rough for a while but I'm doing better now. I'm glad I got some help."

Her gaze flicked to Ben before staring back down at the table. She sat slumped in the booth, ignoring the orange juice and coffee he'd ordered for her.

"Steph," Chase said. "Are you thinking about hurting yourself?"

She turned away from him. "That's not what I want to talk about," she said.

"I thought about it for a while," Chase said, surprising himself. He'd never said that out loud before. He had been thinking about it—before Maggie swept into his life like a hurricane, knocking out all the trash he'd buried himself under. Walking into the house after she'd cleaned out all the liquor bottles had woken him up. And then she wouldn't sleep with him until he resembled something like a sane person. He must be simple-minded, because the sex carrot was what it took to straighten him out, or at least move him away from the cliff.

"I'm not who I used to be," he said. "I've stopped drinking heavily. I'm trying to deal with my shit. You're strong. I know you can do it too."

"I'm not," she said, wiping at her face. Her body trembled.

"You are," he said. "After dinner I'm taking you to the psych ward at the hospital. They're going to help you, Steph. We all need help sometimes."

"No." She shook her head jerkily.

The waitress came over and slid plates of burgers off her

arms and onto the table. Steph didn't take a single bite. He boxed up the food in to-go boxes. Ben's eyes were on Steph, watching her compassionately.

Chase gritted his teeth and forced himself to be patient. Her parents were close by. He'd like to know what the hell they thought about what was happening to her.

"I'll go with you," Ben said. He put down his soda and stared into her eyes. "Let's take our food and go. I was in there a few months ago—it's not bad. They help you to sleep. A couple nights of deep sleep and you'll be halfway there."

Hell, he hadn't realized Ben had been in the psych ward. Chase swallowed and turned his gaze toward the paper receipts on the table. He folded them up and put them in his pocket. People were so damn fragile.

"Do you have a cigarette?" Steph covered her face with a shaking hand.

"I've got two packs. I'll make sure you have cigs while you're in there. Let's go." He stood up and held out his hand to her.

She didn't move, staring at that hand. He held his breath. This vulnerable tearful side of her was new. She'd been cocky and demanding with him. He realized with shame that he hadn't wanted to know more. His throat was tight. His guilt was almost enough to make him capitulate, agree to take care of her and give her what she thought she wanted—him back in her life. They weren't right for each other, but he could stick it out. If it wasn't for Maggie. Well, and if he wasn't also a selfish asshole.

"Let's go, sweetheart," said Ben like the hero he was. "I'm going to help you through this."

Ben took Steph's hand and pulled her to her feet. They walked out of the restaurant without looking back.

∼

CHASE PULLED INTO HIS DRIVEWAY, a tight sinking ache in his chest. He'd been hoping for a miracle. Maggie's van wasn't there. He grabbed his bag from the seat, exhaustion settling over him like a fog.

What had Maggie said—that she was ashamed of herself? That her whole town thought she was a sex worker, and she couldn't stand it. He'd seen red after those assholes had shown up, some ex-boyfriend of hers with his hands all over her.

Then Maggie had thrown up in the side yard, obviously shattered. He'd wanted to pull those dickwads away from her and release his pent-up rage onto their thick heads. Instead, he'd ended up in a serious conversation with Maggie about his intentions. She was walking out the door before he'd had time to gather his thoughts.

He'd said he didn't know what he wanted. That hadn't been right. He wanted Maggie with him. What he couldn't wrap his head around was how they'd been a happy couple forty hours before, and then she'd gotten spooked and decided it wasn't working—but not because of anything he'd actually done. Recently.

He kicked his boots off by the door. He hadn't paid enough attention—they'd been like a couple of honeymooners, and he'd taken it for granted. Then she'd needed him, had just gotten what must have felt like the worst blow of her life, and he'd been too wrapped up in himself to notice.

It dawned on him as he walked into the kitchen that everything was clean and there was a plate of cookies sitting on the counter. He snatched the notepaper from under the plate and snapped it open.

Chase,

Okay, thank you for the work. We need to

renegotiate my salary because I'll be spending less time here. Just during the day while you're working.

Best Wishes,

Maggie

CHAPTER TWENTY

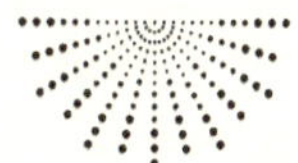

The doorbell chimed. Toto barked and ran out of the kitchen. Maggie's fingers froze on the laptop keys. Nothing good came of answering the door at Chase's house.

Holding her Djucu-nut necklace, she walked to the front door, Toto barking at her side, and inched around to peek out of the tall rectangular window beside the door. She lifted a slat of the blind with her finger. Outside, on the dim front portico was a woman with her back to the door, holding a large package in her arms.

Maggie opened the door. "Hello?"

"Good morning," the woman said, a ball cap with a flower print all over it pulled low over her eyes. "I have a delivery here for"—she paused, glancing down at her clipboard—"Maggie Soloski."

Maggie's eyebrows shot up. "Okay. Do you know who it's from?"

The woman cocked her head. Didn't she get that question all day? "I don't know, but it should say on the card."

"Oh." Maggie automatically took the package when the woman held it out in front of her.

"Enjoy!" the woman called over her shoulder as she jogged down to a flower-print-covered van.

Maggie stood in the doorway, shifting from foot to foot. The box was massive with wide circular holes in the top. A fresh herby potpourri was rising to her face in waves. *Flowers*. She'd never received a delivered bouquet in her life.

In the kitchen, she unwrapped a wide blue vase teeming with flowers spilling over the sides in different colors and shapes, fanning over the top like the proud feathers of a peacock. She stood back, looking at it on the kitchen counter. It transformed the room, jaunty shadows and colors reaching all over the space that surrounded it.

A little envelope was sticking out of the blooms on a glitter-covered wand. She opened it slowly, not wanting to tear the paper.

Maggie, it said, *you're the best thing that's ever happened to me. Chase.*

She huffed, shaking her head. In a daze, she walked over to the couch. She pulled out her cell phone.

> Thank you for the flowers. They're beautiful.

She didn't know what else to say. What else to think.

CHASE

> You're welcome. I want to see you this weekend. You're working early mornings this week so I have to wait. Say yes. Please. Just think about it.

She smiled and covered her face with her hand. The man would do nearly anything to get laid, apparently.

The next day, when the doorbell chimed, there was a different delivery person. A young guy winked at her and held up fifteen balloons and a three-foot teddy bear. The note read, *Don't get used to sleeping alone. You're all I think about. Chase.* She blushed every time she thought about it.

By Friday her fridge was stacked with chocolate-covered strawberries and sparkling wine. There were three massive bouquets in her tiny apartment, an orchid, a mini tree, potted miniature red roses, a hanging "air plant," a basket full of chocolate, a basket of fruit, a box of mixed nuts, snowman brownie pops, a variety pack of coffee, the giant stuffed teddy bear, a miniature plush elephant with a pink bow, and fifteen balloons. The more she told Chase to stop, the more he sent. All his messages, some silly, some romantic, made her think she might have underestimated how much he liked her. Her heart banged against her chest, tired of being ignored. Maybe she should ease up? *You're my girl,* the last one had read. *Do I need to tattoo your name on my bicep?*

Maggie was dream-walking, in a state of constant disbelief. It didn't make sense—unless he was in…She didn't even want to think about the L-word. And yet, every day when she dragged her exhausted feet through her door, there was her collected riot of color and snacks waiting.

Back at her apartment on Friday, with Toto happily worn out from doggie daycare, she stumbled through her front door. The mattress on the floor beckoned her. If she could get a good night's sleep, she'd be able to think. The internship was over, and she didn't have to wake up at two-thirty in the morning again. Face first, she collapsed into the bouncy blow-up mattress, groaning as her muscles began to relax and sink toward the floor. She should at least kick off her shoes. Eat something and shower…

She snapped awake an hour later because her phone buzzed next to her face. She hadn't turned it off before sleeping like she usually did. Not surprising since she still had on her coat. With superhuman effort, she propped herself up on an elbow. The phone stopped ringing. Her balance wobbled, she started sinking back toward the mattress. The phone rang again.

"Hello," she said blearily then realized, with groggy alarm, that she'd forgotten to check the caller id before answering.

"Maggie," said Andy's voice into her ear. "You answered the phone."

"Didn't mean to," she muttered, rubbing her face.

"Were you sleeping? Damn, it's only seven." The phone shuffled around on his end, making friction sounds. She needed a drink. Her hand landed on an empty water bottle. *Dang it.*

"Andy," She began, swallowing against the sandpaper in her throat. Was she getting sick? "I need to go…"

"Wait," Andy cut in. "I want to apologize. And I have some money for you from Princess. I need to tell you about a few things—let me buy you a quick dinner. Or a drink? Anything. I'm here, in the parking lot of your apartment building."

"What?" She shook her head, trying to clear out the fuzz. "You're still in Vegas?"

"Yeah." He laughed nervously. "I'm, um, looking into some job opportunities over here. Music gigs."

"Princess gave you my rent money?" That dang girl. It was like she was doing everything in her power to make trouble.

"Mm hmm, yeah," said Andy. "Come down and talk to me —it's just me. I'm sorry I got Todd involved before. Please come talk to me?"

She pressed on her cheek with one hand, thinking. Her skin felt hot. She put her head down on the cool counter.

"Maggie?"

"I need to go to the store," she said finally. "You can ride with me to grab a few groceries. But I don't like this. You're acting like a stalker."

"No—hey, we're family. I'm worried, that's all. Okay, okay, come down, I'll see you in a minute."

∼

THE DIM PARKING LOT, illuminated by a flickering streetlight, was cold, the wind sharp and piercing through her thin T-shirt. Maggie stopped with her hand on the building's door, considering hiking back up to her apartment for her jacket.

"Hey," said a voice from the bushes to her right. Toto growled.

She jerked back then stumbled. The heavy door swung shut behind her.

"You scared the piss out of me. Why are you in the bushes?"

"Hey, Maggie," Andy said, his face tense. His gaze slid away from hers. He sucked on a cigarette. "Thought I'd be at my car, huh? I'm parked a little way away. You all right? You look run down."

"Gee thanks." She hitched her purse up higher on her shoulder, holding Toto's leash in one hand. "Let's go. I've been up since two in the morning."

"Is that asshole you work for keeping you up all night?"

"What? No. You're all mixed up about what I'm doing." She started walking. Andy followed her after a beat, hands in his pockets.

He cleared his throat. "I'll drive," he croaked. He sounded off—like when he had too many wheels spinning in his head. "I'm wide awake. Lots of coffee today and my car is actually cleanish for once. I don't want to be the straw that breaks the minivan's back." He held up his keys and his newish Corolla beeped back at him cheerfully.

Maggie hesitated, standing on the curb at the edge of the parking lot. She rubbed her eyes. Fatigue pulled at her. Good grief, why had she agreed to this? She picked up Toto. "Just to the grocery store and back. Don't mess with me, Andy."

"Seat warmers, remember?"

She got in and told Andy where to go then leaned back and closed her eyes. The cushy leather upholstery cradled her stiff aching body. The door locks clicked. Andy was uncharacteristically quiet. He didn't even put on angry death metal. Maggie sighed, petting Toto's head. Maybe this wouldn't be so bad.

The turn signals clicked on and off a few times before she roused herself enough to say, "I had an internship in a commercial kitchen, doing pastry." She coughed, trying to clear her scratchy throat. "Crummy hours but it's been a good experience."

"Really?" Andy sounded startled.

"Yeah, really." She forced her eyes open a slit, a little surprised it was taking so long to get to the store.

"I thought you worked for that shithead with the big house."

"I do. He has a construction business and hired me as his personal assistant…" She sat up. They were accelerating onto the freeway. "Where the heck are you going?"

Andy sat hunched over, his face tight and closed off. He kept his eyes on the road, his Adam's apple bobbing as he swallowed.

"Andy," she shouted. "What are you doing?"

Toto barked.

His eyes slid sideways to her then back to the road. "Intervention," he said. "Intervening?"

"Pull over right now."

"I'm on the freeway, I can't pull over."

"Take the next exit then!"

"Listen, listen—just let me explain. I'm doing this because I care. You're family and family takes care of family."

She put her hand down for her cell phone. The cup holder was empty. *Not again.* "Where's my phone?" Her heart beat in her chest like a mixer with too much cookie dough cranked up to max. Her whole body was shaking. She couldn't catch her breath, her chest rising and falling shallowly.

"I've got it—it's safe." Andy gulped. "Hey, calm down for minute…"

Maggie put her head down on the dash, thumping the glove compartment with the flat of her hand. She wanted to launch herself over the gearshift and grab his neck with both hands. Toto barked, jumping and agitated on the floor by her feet.

"Come back to Idaho," Andy shouted. Toto barked louder. "I mean, if not for good then at least for the weekend. If you get away from that shithead for a few days, I think you'll see you don't need to take abuse from anybody. Okay, yeah, that sounds a little hypocritical coming from me right now. But I really care about you. It's different with me."

"Andy, I'm so mad…If you turn the car around right now, I won't get the police involved. Otherwise, this is it—I'm blocking you from my phone, getting a restraining order, whatever the hell it takes."

He chewed on his lip, wiping sweat off his forehead with his hand. "Don't do that, Mags. I'll never be able to get a job with a criminal record. I can't get one now. You wouldn't, like, screw up my whole life just because you're angry, would you? I'll get you back on Sunday for your internship, or whatever, but come to Idaho with me. We can talk—we'll have time to talk, finally. And you can sleep. I'll drive. Obviously."

<h1 style="text-align:center">CHAPTER TWENTY-ONE</h1>

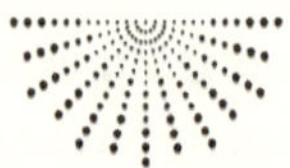

"No." She slammed a fist down on the dash. "No. I will not go to Idaho. This is me telling you no."

"I know you're taking a lot of risks." He tapped his chest, his leg shaking under the steering wheel. "Princess told me you were sleeping in your van in some scuzzy campground for weeks. What the hell was that about?"

She took a deep breath then blew it out slowly. If she had a pen, she would put up a help sign in her window. The only thing in her pockets was a bag of dog treats. She massaged her temples. He needed her to justify herself to him. She clenched her teeth, counting to ten in her head. Then she pulled out Toto's treats, gave him a few, and took a minute to calm him down.

"I camped at Red Rock Canyon, a campground people travel to from all over the country," she said in a tight voice. She leaned back in her chair, Toto on her lap. "Lots of rock climbers and hikers. It was nice. Great view of the mountains."

"Okay," he said. "But why did you go to the brothel in the first place? How could you do—that—to yourself? I mean, shit, Mags, what about the diseases? The creeps that would follow you around—your, um, reputation, I guess. I mean, shit…" His grip was white-knuckled on the steering wheel, his face red.

"You've got the wrong idea about all of it," she said. Even though Andy appeared to be an emo metalhead, with vaguely goth clothing choices, she knew he hadn't totally rejected the extremely conservative views of his family. He had so much guilt and anger, and shame no doubt, about sex and his need for it. *Am I much better?*

"You're not that kind of girl. I mean, yeah, you went through a wild spell after Billy died. But I can't imagine you ever being able to do something like that."

Maggie sighed and swallowed. "Do you have any water in here?" she said.

He looked around, scratching his head. "Shit, no. Damn, I knew I was forgetting something."

"We have to stop for food and drinks," she said. "I haven't eaten anything since this afternoon, and I feel horrible." She covered her throat with a hand. "But no, I couldn't do it. I left the first night and then camped out to save money. From all I've heard, illegal prostitution is horrible and dangerous. But those legal brothels are safer, if you're a person that can deal with sex for money with a lot of different people. There are all these rules, like you always use protection, for everything. The workers see a doctor every week, no matter what. You only work if you're disease-free. One of the people I met in there is a college math teacher. There were all sorts, but everybody was there hoping to make big money. I thought I could make some quick cash to get started with in Vegas."

"So, you're thinking about going back?"

"No. I'm trying to explain to you what it's really like, you idiot. Why, even if I was a legal sex worker, I wouldn't need to be kidnapped. Talking is a better idea—because it isn't a felony."

"You wouldn't talk to me."

"That's your fault." She blew out a breath. The fog of guilt was evaporating inside her. *I'm not ashamed.* Sure, it had been a stupid decision to hare off to Nevada without any savings but it's not like she'd hurt anybody. She'd even landed on her feet, kind of. She sat up a little straighter. "Anyway, I got a different job instead."

"Right," he said sarcastically, "with the shithead. Your employer that you sleep with, like that's not fucked up."

She glanced out the window at the passing lights. *Chase.* Something sweet and tender pulled in her chest. "Well, it makes the workday more fun."

He coughed, glancing over at her. "What, you're actually in love with that asshole?"

The corners of her mouth turned up. "Food, Andy. You promised me dinner and you're going to deliver."

CHASE LEANED against the side of the moving-truck, sweaty and covered in sawdust. Another late Friday working. His empty stomach pinched. That shitty fast-food lunch had been a long time ago.

"How's Steph?" he said to Ben. "Seems like you're helpin' that girl out." She'd been picking him up every night and dropping him off in the morning.

Ben wiped his face off with the inside of his shirt, what looked like an embarrassed flush on his face. "I'm doing more than helping her," he said, grinning. "One of these days she's going to wake up and realize she's too good for me. Until then, I'm gonna make it worth her while."

Chase huffed. "She's lucky to have you. How are the parents?"

Ben crossed his arms. "They're trying, I think. Giving her a hard time but they love her. She wants to get her own place."

"That'd be good for you too." A sleek BMW pulled into the driveway. "Speak of the devil. Head on out, Ben. I'll see you next week."

Chase pulled the sliding door down to close the back of the truck full of his equipment. It closed with the usual crash and snap as the metal locking mechanism swung into place.

He glanced at his phone. Still nothing from Maggie. She'd probably crashed for the night. He sighed. He'd like to crawl in next to her.

ANDY PULLED into a drive-through fast-food line. "Let's order a ton," he mumbled around the unlit cigarette in his mouth. "Hard to find anything open headed north—hey, Maggie!"

Maggie opened the passenger door and stepped out of the car onto black asphalt, carrying Toto. A barrier of shrubs blocked the drive-through lane from the street. Cars were in front and back of them, waiting. She edged along the curb to get by Andy's car.

"Maggie, wait." Andy stood next to his door. "Where are you going?"

The cars in front of them shifted forward, opening up the drive-through lane. She crossed through, not looking back at Andy. The car behind him pressed on its horn and flashed its lights. She opened the door into the restaurant and ducked inside.

She blinked, letting her eyes adjust to the bright orange and red interior. There were a handful of people at the tables.

She crossed in front of the counter, ignoring the glare she got from a woman at the register as she headed toward the bathrooms. At the end of a small hallway, she stopped. On the bathroom door was painted *for customers only*. There was a key code lock on the door.

Head aching, she leaned against the wall. She pushed up and propelled herself to an empty booth at the back of the restaurant. A baby cried pitifully. She put Toto down on the seat next to her and then slumped forward onto her arms.

"Maggie." Andy slid into the booth across from her. "Hey, let's get some dinner then keep going. You can lean that seat back and fall asleep. What do you want, chicken or beef?"

"Andy," she said with her mouth against her elbow. "I'm not getting in that car again unless I'm driving."

He ran his hands through his hair, his knee bumping against the bottom of the table. "You'll feel better once you eat." He stood up and went to the counter.

She massaged her temples. Her fury with him had passed and now she was as limp as a boiled piece of bare pasta. He was clinging to her, trying to be a part of her life, compulsively concerned about what she was doing.

Andy made expansive hand gestures as he ordered their dinner, the woman at the register smiling into her collar. People usually thought he was high on drugs, but it was just him, churning out enough energy to power a small city.

A doctor had prescribed something to help him with his mania, but he didn't take it. He'd said it dampened down the world too much. In some way, he had depended on her to regulate him. She was the person who listened to him, and vice versa. They used to have routines: movie on Thursday, football on Sunday. He'd hung around during her work shifts, smoking out back with the dishwasher then drinking coffee and eating donuts next to the waitress station. On Tuesdays they'd walked through the thrift stores downtown,

Maggie looking for kitchen equipment or clothes, Andy marginally interested in musical odds and ends. He'd been there waiting for her at the end of her shift, pacing in the alley behind the old diner. He'd been her best friend.

He was willing to do anything, apparently, to keep her in his life. And everything he did made it worse. But he kept on trying. Despite herself, she was touched.

He needed to go back to college, get out in the world and limit the time he spent alone. An idea bubbled to the surface of her tired brain. If she did it, she was acknowledging that she cared and wasn't going to cut him out of her life.

She blew out a breath. A week ago, she'd been determined to totally start over, not be tied to anyone who knew about all the mistakes she'd made. But maybe she couldn't do that. *I don't want to.*

Andy slid a milkshake, a soda, and a water in front of her. She raised her eyebrows. The cold soda tamped down the fire burning in her throat.

"I know you're thirsty, sorry about that," he said. As if her being thirsty was the worst thing about the entire situation. "I told them Toto was a certified emotional support dog. I think they'll look the other way."

"Andy, I want to take you somewhere. Give me your keys."

CHAPTER TWENTY-TWO

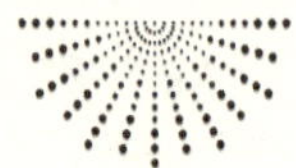

Chase's phone rang. He put the call on speaker. "Howdy," he said. "Why the hell are you calling me on a Friday night? Your girl leave you?"

"Chase Montgomery," his brother Buck said, "I had to make sure you were still breathin'. My girl's fine. You're the one who skipped Christmas at the ranch again this year. What the hell's happening with you?"

Chase sniffed. The dark empty house he was squatting in pretty much summed up his life at the moment. He leaned back in Maggie's office chair, staring out the window at the lights around the pool. "I'm workin'. Busting my ass getting this business off the ground. Swinging a hammer's a busy gig out here. How's your new resort?"

"Comin' along. All the cabins are rented out. Lodge is getting finished, flooring going in this week. We're all missing your sour face so there's talk about a trip. And everybody knows about the pool."

"Shit."

"You're living in a big empty house, with a vacation in the

backyard, and you haven't invited anybody over. What the hell are you thinkin'?"

Chase fired off his last email, clicking on the auto signature Maggie had created. "The place is torn up. I'm flipping it, not hosting parties."

"I heard, and I'm not sayin' any names, that there's a pretty blonde in your life these days."

"Fucking Lucas."

"Come on now, spill it."

Chase glanced over at the cake Maggie had made for him. It had pineapple, cherries, and caramelly stuff on top and around the sides with two layers of whipped cream in the middle. It was spongy and sweet. He'd already had two slices. "She's not sure she can put up with me."

Buck snorted. "Smart woman."

Chase sighed. "I'm in the middle of my metamorphosis into becoming a henpecked sad old cock. You and Austin infected me with this settling down bullshit. To hell with both of ya and your damn happy little families."

"Holy shit. Well, that settles it, we're comin' out to meet her."

"House'll be done in a month. Maybe by then Maggie will have had mercy on me."

"Always thought you needed a tough one. There's my girl —I better go on over there and get her attention. Chase, do somethin' nice, for a change, and let your poor girl feel some love. I'm gonna look at flights." Buck hung up.

Chase stood up and stretched. It had been a long week. He'd been putting in twelve-hour days so that he could clear out time to spend with Maggie. Really get them straightened out this weekend. Instead, she wasn't buying his bullshit.

He huffed. Buck had said the L-word. *Love.* He rubbed his eyes. The best thing would be to start over with her and meet her when he wasn't at rock bottom. *Too late for that.* She'd left a note thanking him again for the gifts he'd sent to her, but she still hadn't agreed to see him this weekend.

His phone buzzed with an incoming text message. He flipped it open and read.

MAGGIE

Having a crazy night and I need your help. Again—sorry about that. I'm taking my friend Andy to the Dirty Rabbit. Can you meet me there? He sort of kidnapped me but I've got the keys now. I'll explain everything later.

"WHERE ARE YOU TAKING US?" Andy drummed out a beat on his leg, an unlit cigarette hanging out of his mouth.

She'd refused to tell him the last two times he'd asked. She took the exit for Pahrump. "You've been one hundred percent out of line this last month. I'm never going to forgive you. But I think I might keep being your friend if you change your ways and try something tonight."

"Wait, this is that town—fuck, Maggie. Why are you taking us here?"

She parked in front of the Dirty Rabbit. "Because, if we both experience this place, you might stop holding it against me. We'll be on level footing again. Also, it might mellow you the freak out."

He snorted. "Princess tried. I mean we did a little—but I thought, I don't know, like it was too…"

"Hey, I really don't need to know about it."

He bit on a fingernail. With a grunt, he opened his door then jumped out and lit his cigarette. Toto followed him. Andy leaned down so his head could peer in the cab at her. "You think this shit is all right?"

She sniffed, gathering up her things. "I don't know. It

wasn't right for me." She tossed him his car keys then got out. Toto trotted back to her side and she put him on his leash.

Andy paced back and forth next to his car. She knew he wasn't a virgin but there hadn't been much happening for him in small conservative Ridgeview, Idaho.

She sneezed. "Come on," she said, nasally. "Let's go get a drink." Without looking back, she started walking toward the entrance.

He muttered something, closed the car door, then hustled up beside her. "Shit, Maggie, I don't know about this."

The women loved Toto. He stood on his hind legs and waved his front paws, licked fingers, and made happy snuffles and grumbly growls. "It's Toto," one of the older women squealed. She had her picture taken with Toto held up against her face.

Andy stuck close to Maggie's side, compulsively messing with his hair. Finally, she dragged him over to the bar and got him drinking. She ordered a hot toddy, almost tearful at the relief drinking it gave her sore throat.

"I'm surprised they let Toto in here," Andy said, nursing his second shot of Jägermeister.

"Me too." Maggie watched a pretty, dark-skinned woman with a determined expression walk toward them. "Here's your date. Relax, she's going to handle everything, if you want. I'll be next door at the burger bar. See you."

"Maggie—" He grabbed her elbow, but she slipped away. At the exit, she glanced back and saw the tall woman rubbing his shoulders.

The burger bar was busy, but she found an empty table and sat down. She pulled her phone out and saw a message from Chase.

CHASE

WTF? I'm going to kill that asswipe. Hang tight, I'm leaving now.

She cradled the phone against her chest. Was she doing this? Getting back together with him right where they'd started? She closed her eyes. *I am afraid.* He'd accused her of running scared and he was right.

There was a voice mail from Princess. She pressed play, putting the phone next to her aching head.

"Hey, girlfriend. Listen, don't be mad about the whole Andy thing. He has, like, so much energy I didn't even know what to do with him. He told me about some crazy plan, and I said yes just to get him out of my hair, you know? Anyway, you can handle him. I sort of told him about you working at the Dirty Rabbit one night when we were drunk. But I have good news. That sleazy old lawyer you owe money, I took care of that fucker for you. He's, like, totally in my pocket now. I made him write out a receipt for you. Your debt is clear. You're welcome. Now we're even—and he did a bunch of stuff for me with the divorce and restraining order. Fucking fabulous. I'm going to look into law school, I'd totally kick ass at that shit. All right, I'm leaving tomorrow. Back to making bank at the Rabbit. The house key will be under that rock. Love ya."

CHAPTER TWENTY-THREE

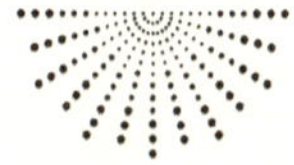

Chase walked in the burger bar and spotted Maggie right away with her head down on the table. Toto was eating something off the ground by her feet. He stomped over to her.

"Where is he?"

She startled, sitting up fast, then pressed a hand to her head. "Do you have to shout?"

He scowled at her. "What's the matter with you?"

"Tired. Headache."

He sat next to her. "Tell me where he is so I can kill him. Then everything will be fine."

She leaned her head against his shoulder. "I want you to leave it alone. It's handled. I'm staying friends with him, even though he's an idiot."

"What? After everything he's done—"

"Hey, stop hulking out."

He closed his eyes and counted to ten. Then he did it again. She kissed his shoulder. He sat up straighter. "Fine."

Toto jumped up onto his lap. The little dog sniffed at him then flopped on his side. Chase yawned.

"Let's go," Maggie said, not moving.

He grunted. "Come on, woman. I have a surprise for you."

She groaned. "I'm so tired."

The three of them shuffled outside. He took her hand, guiding her toward the long line of suites the Dirty Rabbit rented out for the night. There was an outdoor bench with a view of the desert. A full moon rose overhead. Toto explored a creosote bush with intense interest.

Chase sat down, pulling Maggie onto his lap. She settled against him, putting her head down on his shoulder. His heart beat hard against his chest. *Say it, you damn coward.*

"Before you pass out on me—"

"I have not been drinking."

"I know. Listen to me, babe. I realized something today. It's been there for a while, but I guess it took you being hard on me for it to penetrate my thick skull." He glanced down at her face, turned up toward his. Her expression was puzzled. He squeezed her hands tighter.

"I'm a difficult beast. Short tempered. Messy. I drink too much and you're probably going to want me to go spew shit about my feelings to some uptight asshole with a PhD attached to their name…"

"Chase, what are you talking about?"

He took a deep breath. Her eyes were dark and opaque as he stared down into them. "I realized today that I love you, Maggie. You're it for me."

"What?" She blinked, her eyebrows pinched together.

"I love you." His mouth quirked up at the total bewilderment on her face.

"You love me?"

"I don't want to fuck around. I realized today I had to tell you because we need to be together. I don't deserve someone like you so all I can do is offer you the best that I have. I'm going to offer that when we're not at the Dirty Rabbit—because that's a tricky thing to explain about at dinner parties."

She sat up, a hand on her head. "I don't believe you."

He hugged her, kissing her temple. "We never would have found each other if you hadn't come here. Thank God you tried being a sex worker."

She stood up and took a few steps away from him. "What about you feeling like I was putting a gun to your head because I wanted to talk about the future?"

"Hey, I can build shit. I never claimed I wasn't an idiot."

"You realized today? So you were sending me all of those gifts before you felt that?"

"I think I started feeling it the first time I saw you," he said. "I don't completely know why."

She snorted.

"I mean I could hardly think through the lust fog but there you were. Brave." He shrugged. "Ambitious. Tough. You were under my skin from the jump."

She pressed a shaking hand to her chest.

He leaned forward. "I know I'm rushing here but my gut is telling me this is right. We both need to settle down and be permanently connected to each other. Be safe, grounded, and all that…stuff. You, me, and our ugly little dog. I'm joking—his looks have grown on me and now, when I see him, I don't think rat but instead furry little buddy. Will you come over here and hug me?"

"Wait." She put out a hand. "You're telling me you know this, but it's only been one day."

He smiled at her. Toto jumped up on the bench next to him and leaned on his side. Maggie put a hand over her eyes and gulped out a sob. She walked forward and hugged him.

"I love you too," she croaked.

"Come on." He pulled her toward their suite. "Lie down. I'll run to the store and buy you cold medicine."

~

MAGGIE WOKE UP SLOWLY, convinced she was still dreaming —of herself in a strange hotel room. Her hand landed on a piece of paper on top of the rumpled pillow next to her.

*I took Toto out to let you sleep and to find some breakfast. Call me when you're awake.
Love, Chase.*

She sat up, rubbing her face. A lot had happened. Chase loved her? She stumbled into the bathroom.

A little while later she heard the outside door open and Toto bark. He scratched at the bathroom door.

"Hey, buddy," she called.

"Mornin'," Chase said, on the other side of the door. "How are you feeling?"

"Better, I think. Going to get in the shower."

"Can I scrub your back?"

She grinned. The man was addicted to his morning grind. "Fine. If we don't use this couple's shower, we aren't getting our money's worth."

He came in and kissed her. She tasted coffee and donuts and him. A twist in her middle sent warmth out to her fingers and toes. "Hey, I don't want to get you sick."

He picked her up off the floor and hugged her. "I'll be fine. Damn, woman, I missed you this last week."

She inhaled, her chest constricting as she thought about losing him. What if it didn't work out? How could he know?

"Me too," she whispered.

"Hey," he said, pulling back to cup both sides of her face. "We're going to be happy, Maggie. We can do it." His eyes were crinkled up at the corners, the flecks of green bright among the layers of brown and gold.

"I'm not sure I know how." She sniffed, her nose stinging.

"Same way you do anything. One step at a time." He kissed her again. "Come on, we're way overdue for our wake and wiggle."

They both really liked the shower. Chase said he was taking notes for their future bathroom suite. She blinked at him, startled.

They checked out. Maggie saw Andy's car still in the parking lot. She sent him a text as they pulled onto the highway.

"So, what's the deal with the idiot?" Chase sniffed, gripping the steering wheel. "Why aren't we filing a police report?"

Maggie turned onto her side on the reclined seat, petting Toto with one hand. "I mean, he's a unique person. What he did was wrong even if his heart was in the right place, sort of. I don't have many people in my life."

He huffed. "Damn leech. What happens now?"

"I guess he's moving out here." Toto licked her hand. Chase scowled. "He should have left Ridgeview a long time ago and found a music gig. Vegas seems right for him, if he can land on his feet."

Chase scratched his chin. "You could sublet your apartment to him."

She blinked. "Wait, are you saying you want to start living together right away…"

He frowned at her. "Of course I do. We'll go pick up your stuff today."

"Wow." She rolled onto her back and stared at the ceiling of the truck. Her mind was paralyzed while her heart did high kicks in her chest. He really didn't want to wait.

His hand grabbed hers above Toto's head. "You're too far away when we aren't sleeping together every night. It's too quiet without you and Toto bustling around. And when you take another internship, I'll get our fur kid here to daycare."

"Yeah?"

"Hell yes." He squeezed her hand. "My stalker ex has moved on."

"How do you know?"

"She's dating Ben. He even talked her into the psych ward at the hospital for a power nap. I'm gonna keep my distance but my gut tells me I'm clear."

She pulled her hand out of his. "Let me think for a bit. You're treating us like a project deadline—I'm about three steps behind you."

"Don't forget about the pool, babe." He winked at her.

She smiled, covering her face with her hands. "You're unreal. What happened to the Chase I met, what, seven weeks ago? The guy who went to brothels and sought out lots of casual sex?"

He put his arm across the back of the seat. "I started thinking rationally, that's what. The serious answer is, you met me on the anniversary of my buddy's death. It's always a bad time for me but the ex-girlfriend stalker pushed me over the edge. And I was alone too much—I'm not used to that. Work stress got to me a bit too, I guess. Then I met you. You flipped my pancake and cooked my sausage in a way that hit me as hard as a frying pan."

"I've almost hit you with a frying pan a couple times."

"All the gushy love stuff aside, my dumb brain clued into the math. Couples have more sex. A lot more—especially workaholics like me. It was like a lightbulb switched on in my brain."

She snorted and pressed on her temples. The big truck rumbled below her, lulling her eyes closed.

She wrapped her fingers around her Djucu-nut necklace. There was no way to truly know who a person was after seven weeks. She'd experienced that with every single one of her ex-boyfriends. They had been sweet in the beginning, with plans for their futures, and exciting things happening in their lives. Then she'd see them snap at their mothers, casually treat a server like trash, blow a paycheck, become a belligerent drunk, or simply be too self-absorbed to ask her a single question. Here she was, gambling again, on the moodiest, most short-tempered man she'd ever taken a chance on.

Chase drove silently next to her, letting her rest. He was a handful and yet she thought he was one of the more honest people she'd ever been close to—about himself, anyway. *Who does he think I am?*

A little while later, her phone jolted her out of a light doze. Toto growled. She sat up and answered.

"Maggie, where are you? I texted you last night and never heard back."

"I'm with Chase. My boyfriend."

Next to her, Chase grunted.

"Oh." It sounded like Andy was pacing on gravel and smoking. "Can you hang out today? Fuck, there's so much we need to talk about."

She adjusted the strap of her flip-flop and took a deep breath. "No. I have plans with Chase. I'm working a lot, in kitchens and with the construction business."

Andy gulped something. "Listen, I'm sorry. I keep fucking up. I'll do better—I've been going batshit in that town without you there. I tried going off my meds and it's like a tornado hit my life. Damn it."

Maggie glanced at Chase. He glared back at her, his eyebrows drawn together. *Oh, what the heck.* "Okay, I have an idea. Chase's actually. I'm going to talk to my apartment complex office about subletting my studio to you. If they say yes, pick up the key in the office."

"Wait, what about you?"

"I'm moving in with Chase."

CHAPTER TWENTY-FOUR

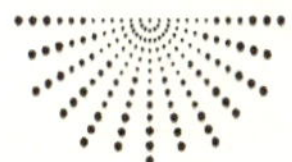

"Hey, honey, I'm home." Chase stomped into the kitchen and dropped his lunch cooler on the counter. "What is that thing, a donut tower?"

"It's a croquembouche, which means something that crunches in the mouth. It's French."

"Huh. Can I knock it over?"

"It's for my blog portfolio. If you break a single caramel swirl, I'll—oh, no, don't you kiss me now. You're covered in plaster dust. Get out of my kitchen."

"Babe, that apron is hot. Crunchy hot. You think you can hurt me with that little spatula?"

Toto barked while jumping in circles around them. Chase ran out of the kitchen in mock terror. His head popped back around the corner. "Before I forget, you need to buy a nice dress. And hiking gear. And anything else. In the next two days."

"What?"

He tossed a credit card down on the counter. "Use that. It's all part of the gig. There will be pictures taken so do all the things."

"That doesn't explain anything."

"Gotta go." He disappeared into the bathroom.

She picked up the card and stared at her name on the front. He wanted her to buy clothes? *I'll pay him back.* Yeah, sure she would.

Teeth gritted and muscles clenched, she fought the bone-deep longing for cute fresh clothes. And lost. She put the credit card carefully in her wallet. Working on houses had destroyed most of her meager wardrobe—the truth was, she didn't have the willpower to resist a golden ticket. She blew out a breath. The more she learned about Chase and the business the more she realized he was making big money. At least, the numbers he juggled around like they were nothing were huge to her.

The next afternoon, Andy picked her up to go shopping. It was the first time she'd seen him since the Dirty Rabbit trip almost two weeks before. He'd agreed to let her drive because it was the only way she'd get in a car with him.

"Thanks for seeing me, Mags," he said, fingers combing his hair.

She tossed a sandwich at him. "Eat that. You look like you've lost weight."

He shrugged. "My appetite's gone now that I'm back on my meds."

She drove them toward the big REI store for her outdoor gear. "How's your job hunt?"

"Got my Nevada driver's license this week. Planning to get a food-handlers permit tomorrow. I've been looking around, called a few places. The sound engineer program you told me about ain't too bad—I went over there and had a tour. I think I'll work at whatever and get started on that shit."

"Nice. How's the apartment?"

"Fine, I guess. Getting to know the other smokers.

They're all right." He took a bite of his sandwich. "What about you?"

"I'm applying to a few cooking competitions. There's a Hell's Kitchen here, did you know? A couple other ones film in Vegas. Plus, LA is only four hours away."

"Damn, that shit's brutal."

"How much worse can it be than Marlene's Diner in Ridgeview? She was like Gordon Ramsey on steroids and cranked out on meth."

He huffed. "Yeah. She misses you. Asked me about you every week."

"Huh."

"The thing with your prick is going good, I guess."

"Geez, what a nice thing to say."

"Whatever. You know what I mean."

"It is." She turned into the parking lot. "Too good. It makes me nervous."

"The dude came out of nowhere."

"He has parents. A couple of brothers too, over in Oregon. We video-chatted with them a few days ago. It was weird. They're all nice people—ranchers. I've never met anyone's parents through a Skype call before."

Andy slumped in his seat. "Does he know you're out with me today?"

She blinked, then pulled into a parking spot and turned off the car. "Yeah, of course he does."

"He seemed, like, short tempered and possessive."

"I told him you're my friend, and it isn't negotiable. He was angry about the kidnapping. But he's all bark and no bite. Pretty considerate man, really, to the people he cares about."

Andy smiled at her. "He's gonna have to put up with me."

She nodded her head at him. "As long as I do. Come on.

Chase talked me into spending some of his money and I'm too greedy to turn him down."

~

MAGGIE BOUGHT a semi-formal dinner dress with long sleeves, a deep V-neckline, and a skirt that hit her at mid-thigh. The material was a navy-blue floral jacquard. A pair of heeled riding boots completed her outfit. The look was a little casual but, in Vegas, she'd pass.

Saturday morning, Chase was his usual extremely amorous self except there was something more. He kept hugging her.

"Damn, you're cute," he said, grabbing her from behind in the kitchen. "I didn't think pants with zippers around the knees could be so hot. And this tank top..." He groaned, kissing the back of her neck.

Heat flared up and down her skin. "Oh—but what about the schedule you've been drilling me about all morning?"

He pushed her front against the kitchen counter, grabbing her hips and pumping against her backside. "Drilling —yes."

His phone rang, rattling on the counter next to them. He groaned, then picked it up and answered. "Yeah?" His arm slid away from her waist as he listened. He took a step back. "Fine. Yes, we'll be there." He hung up, rubbing his face. "Damn it, we've got to go."

Maggie smoothed down her clothing. "When are you going to tell me what's going on?"

His mouth quirked up. "In about forty minutes."

She fiddled with her makeup during the short drive. "Are you getting photos for your website or something? Or social media?"

"They're photos for us. I want a nice screen saver for my

phone of the two of us. And, I need to document how good I look right now before the potbelly sets in."

"I doubt you'll ever slow down long enough for one of those." She grinned at him. He did look good. His face scruff was trimmed up and he'd gotten a haircut. A white linen short-sleeved shirt casually showed off broad shoulders and powerful arms.

He winked at her. "If I do, you'll have to only make me one cake a week instead of two. Going to stick with pastry long term? If you do, I'll have to bite the bullet and buy a workout bike."

She stared out at the approaching cliffs. "I'm not sure. Lately I'm more interested in learning about all of it. But, you know, my background's humble. I can whip up diner food with one hand behind my back, but fine dining is another beast. You can't just read about those dishes, you have to taste them too. How can you be innovative with black truffle oil when you've never even smelled it? I don't know. I'm in my head about it."

"You'll get there. I don't deserve to be with a chef but that's how it shakes out sometimes." He parked the truck. "Come on, sugar, we've got an hour of walking ahead of us."

"Is this the Calico Tanks Trail?"

"It is. Two point two miles."

"Do you think I'm a wimp or something? That's a stroll, not a hike."

Their feet crunched on the ground, red dust whirling up around their hiking boots. "If you want to explore the whole canyon, we'll get there. It's almost two hundred thousand acres of land so it'll keep us busy for a while."

They climbed up the trail as the morning warmed up into the low fifties. Chase, it turned out, was a trivia guy interested in everything from the news to geology. He pointed out plant species, and what kind of rock they were looking at.

"Ever thought about going into science?" she said after he wound down from a talk about the composition of limestone.

"I'd rather read about it. Doing the dirty work suits me—keeps me movin'. And I like the money." He grinned at her.

They topped a rise and the brown Mojave Desert stretched out below them with the city of Vegas a sea of gray and blue. Maggie leaned forward, bracing her hands on her knees while her heart pumped. "Turns out coming straight up is a little challenging." They drank out of their water bottles. Even Toto seemed tired.

Chase put his backpack down on a rock. He took her hands, scowling.

"Are you okay?" she asked.

He huffed. "My heart's beating too fast. Don't worry, I'm fine. I'm going to ask you something—even though it's too soon."

Her eyes were wide. "Okay. You know I'll answer any questions you have about me. I'm not keeping any secrets."

His mouth opened and closed, a smile pulling at the edges. "Shit, you really don't suspect me at all?"

"Of what?"

When he laughed, she pulled her hands away and put them on her hips.

"No, sorry, give me those hands back. Okay. I'm a little nervous, that's all."

"Nervous?"

"Maggie, I love you. I love us, together. I've lost people I cared about and it taught me something—that I don't want to waste time. I want to build our life together. We'll both be better off in every way if you'll settle down with me. You saw me at my worst and in a weird way I'm glad that it was you who found me there. From now on I'm going to show you my best and try every day to be the man you deserve. See, I'm already cussing less."

He sank to his knees in front of her. Someone was taking pictures of them. Toto barked at the camera person and Chase told him to sit then petted his head. He looked back up at her. She couldn't breathe. Was he out of his mind?

"Marry me, Maggie. Let's take care of each other."

"Chase, I didn't see this coming—I'm not ready…How can you…I mean, I haven't even met your family."

His mouth quirked up. "It's okay. I knew I'd take you by surprise. My family is coming when we finish the house. I'm hoping to have sweetened you up by then so we can have a Vegas wedding while they're here." He sniffed. "We could even invite your scumbag best friend, if you want to."

She pulled him up to his feet. "I love you. You don't have to marry me to keep me around, you know."

"Uh-huh. Thank you." He waved to the photographer. "We'll see you tonight."

"What's happening tonight?"

"We're going on a date."

CHAPTER TWENTY-FIVE

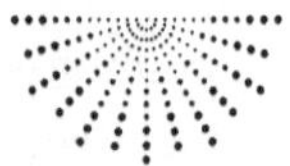

Chase stared at Maggie in the dark blue dress. She smiled shyly up at him, putting a hand on one hip. "Did I clean up all right?"

"More than all right. I'd kiss you but then I'd be wearing lipstick. Come on, beautiful, we're doing another photo session before dinner."

"Will you please explain it to me now? What's your plan with the photographs?"

He kissed her hand instead of her mouth. She hadn't said yes to him, and he was doing his best not to hold it against her. "Get in the truck and I'll tell you as we drive."

"So," she said as they drove toward the strip. "What's your plan? I know you have one."

"Is that vanilla perfume? You're a walking cookie." He shifted in his seat. The woman drove him crazy, even after a long afternoon of pinning her down in bed. Especially after.

"Cookie? You're getting hungry."

"Always, when you're around." He smoothed down the front of his shirt. "The photos are for a few things. Working on houses, I see a lot of different decorating. One of the things I like are family photos, done by a pro. It's cheesy, vain, sometimes tacky, but when I think about home, I want that stuff on the walls. Pictures of us. There was only one chance to record today, and I made it happen."

She put a hand on his shoulder, gliding her fingers up to rub the back of his neck. He leaned into her touch. "You keep surprising me. I wouldn't have guessed you were sentimental."

"My family is everything to me."

"I like those photos too."

The truck rumbled over the highway as he moved through traffic toward the downtown strip. *Say it.* He'd made assumptions but it was time to dig deeper. "Do you want family life? Are you ready for it?"

She dropped her hand. "I do want it—it's what I've always wanted."

He exhaled and forced himself to stay quiet.

She stared away from him, out the passenger window. "I thought I'd marry my high school sweetheart. We spent five years together, on and off. His parents really took me in. I wanted to be a part of their family more than anything. Then I realized I hadn't seen him clearly. And it's happened every other time—it's fun and hot in the beginning and then, sooner or later, there's this moment when Toto pulls back the curtain and you see the wizard for what he is. Totally different than you thought."

"Toto is a damn smart dog."

"I've only had my Toto for about a year and a half. That was confusing, wasn't it?" She huffed. "You're the first guy that my Toto's actually liked."

"I get that though, not trustin' yourself to read people. My problem is, I don't trust anyone. Always seeing the worst. In the military I had to make snap judgments about who could handle things and if I was wrong, at the least, bad shit happened. Often wrong, never in doubt, went through my head because I had to do it. It's harder to see who people are in civilian life."

She glanced at him. "Don't you worry about our, um, overworked hoo-hahs shading how we see things? Yeah, yeah, go ahead and laugh, but I mean, hon, I've never had so much nooky in my life. I can't think straight. That's an important piece, sure, but I'm not sure you recognize me past it."

He turned into a parking garage and then had to jump out to buy a ticket. Back inside the truck he said, "You aren't wrong. It's more and better nooky than I've ever had either and it's burning me up. Like winning the lottery." He smiled. "I was a little obsessed with what I thought of as hot sex, especially these last couple of years. Now it all seems hollow." He pulled into a spot and turned off the truck.

"Huh. I thought we were having hot sex."

He brushed his lips across hers then pulled back. "Love makes it better. I don't think there are many people I could love. You're the one for me. Come on, we have an appointment at the Bellagio Fountains."

MAGGIE FOUND herself on the kind of date that could only happen in Vegas. They started at the Bellagio Fountains Show outside. A photographer took photos of Chase whirling her around in his arms while thousands of jets shot water up four hundred and sixty feet and a loudspeaker bellowed out Frank Sinatra's 'Somewhere Beyond The Sea.' Water mist coated her skin and she shivered.

"Time for a hot dinner," Chase said. "We're going to the Eiffel Tower."

The restaurant was on the eleventh floor of the half-sized

replica of the French tower. Their table was right next to a window with the fountains below them.

"Wow," she squeaked, a wide grin on her face. "This is amazing."

He winked at her. "And the steak is good too."

She opened the menu and scanned the prices. She closed it and set it down. "Oh, good Lord."

Chase waved his hand around in the air. "Don't worry. And order whatever you're the most interested in tasting. I'm tryin' the Wellington."

She went with the venison. It was an extremely difficult decision. Chase asked the server to take their photo and she plastered a smile on her face, sitting up very straight, wondering if her wide-eyed shock would show.

After they had wine, and bread, and a few interesting pates to try on the table, Maggie cleared her throat. It was a day for big conversations. Knots tightened in her chest—this question seemed like a cliff.

"You asked me earlier, in the truck, if I was ready for family life. I have a question for you as well." She took a sip of her wine.

"Lay it on me, babe."

She huffed. "All right. Well, when I realized my life wasn't going to end up with my own family in the town I grew up in, and that I didn't want to stay there anyway, I made plans. Becoming a chef is grueling and the hours are horrible. Also, I've entered a few cooking competitions. If I get into them, I'll be traveling and living close to the set during filming."

"Hell's Kitchen?" His face screwed up and he shook his head. "I hate that pompous asshole."

"That's one of them. At least they're local."

"If he makes you cry, I'll kill him."

She sighed and pressed her smile flat. "If I'm lucky enough to get on any cooking show, it will be a miracle. My point is, my career and family life don't match up in my head, at the moment."

He leaned back in his chair. "Oh. You mean kids other than our fur baby?"

She blinked at him. "You look a little shocked."

He put his hands up. "I said kids and my balls shriveled up."

"Um…"

He chuckled. "Hey, don't worry. We'll get there. Right now wouldn't be a great time for either of us but whatever happens we'd handle it together." He drummed his fingers on the table for a few beats. "I don't know how to say this without sounding like an asshole but I'm going to be honest. I'm hoping you won't mind living rough and light for a bit while the business builds. If we can flip houses for a few years, we'll get a nice boost."

"Huh." She wouldn't mind that.

"As for the cooking shows and all of it, I get it. I work long horrible hours too. Both of us are maniacs. We're perfect for each other."

They ended the night with a gondola ride at the Venetian Hotel. Maggie leaned back against Chase's chest as they floated along the artificial canal, under bridges and past cafes, their driver belting out an Italian song.

She gripped his hand. Life with Chase was a bit like waking up and finding herself in the Technicolor land of Oz. Sooner or later she'd have to go back to the real world.

CHAPTER TWENTY-SIX

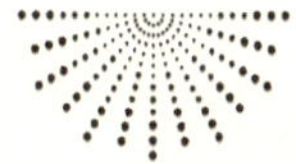

Maggie spent the next two weeks working on The Pool House.

"It's a turn-key buy," Chase said while they took a lunch break late during the second week.

"Somebody's going to pay all of that extra money just so they don't have to lift a finger after they move in?"

"You bet they will. And plenty of buyers want everything brand new. All the crap in here was over twenty years old in any case, so it was due."

Chase had gutted the interior. Even the stair railings went so he could put in black metal ones that matched the new ebony oak front door. Every inch of the kitchen was different, from the cabinetry to the appliances. It smelled like a new car in there.

She sighed. "I hope it all gets reused. Makes me bluesy."

He put his head in her lap. She jumped as he nudged up her shirt with his nose. "I've got you, babe," he mumbled against her stomach.

"Wait," she whispered, pushing at his head. "Your crew is in the other room."

"Oh yeah." He rolled off her. "Wanna race upstairs?"

"We're on a deadline," she said, trying to sound stern. They'd moved into the finished bedroom suite the week before. He'd sweet-talked her in there for day quickies more than once and she was becoming a convert. "That staging company you hired is going to show up with their moving truck of furniture in two days. How are we going to finish everything?"

He put an arm over his eyes. "We'll get there."

Miraculously, he was right. There was still a laundry list of things to wrap up, but the big stuff was done. The furniture and decorations were moved in, transforming The Pool House into a completely furnished home, with a high-end vacation rental kind of vibe.

Friday evening, Maggie walked around with her bottle of glass cleaner and a microfiber rag to touch up the windows. Mostly, she marveled.

Chase walked up to her, scowling at his phone. There had been a lot of back and forth with his brother Buck about a visit. Apparently, his family was coming.

She turned to him, smiling. "Holy fireworks, Batman, this place is done."

"Yeah," he said, "it is. Now everyone wants to come over here and mess it up. Some cheap tickets popped up. They're flying in tomorrow."

"What—wow. Okay."

He sighed, shoving his phone into his back pocket. "I told them to rent a damn car but the whole crew is coming. Buck, Randi, Austin, Ellie, their rugrats, and my parents. Jesus."

Her stomach flipped over. She glanced out the window at her Mini-V. Would Chase forgive her if she disappeared and went camping instead?

~

CHASE WOKE UP EARLY, managing to silence his alarm before Maggie did more than turn over. He stared at her naked back, blonde curls spread out on the pillow next to her head. The beast stirred inside him, ready to pounce.

Instead, he swung his feet off the mattress. She was rattled about meeting his family and needed to sleep. She'd suggested that she could leave last night, for the weekend, and give him time to catch up with everyone. He'd nearly lost it. Perhaps he wasn't as recovered as he liked to pretend he was.

He grabbed his clothes and phone and headed to the downstairs shower so he wouldn't wake her up. The hot water pounded down on him, clearing out the last of the sleep fog clouding his head.

The auction started in three hours. There were three rehab properties he wanted to take another look at before bidding. Between the auction and putting in a few hours at the new build construction site, he'd barely make it back in time to meet his family if he rushed. Maggie would hold it against him if he left her on her own with them for too long.

She might not be ready for marriage—she definitely wasn't sure about him. The ring boxes were hidden upstairs in his briefcase. He turned off the water and pulled his towel down from the shower door. The girl should pull her head out of the sand and take advantage of what he was offering. What did she have to lose? He was the one who could be scalped out of half his assets.

He thought of Jake and Marcus, who both had girlfriends mourning them. They might be a little proud of him. There were a hundred selfish reasons he wanted to marry Maggie and a few reasons that might be chalked up as good. His money would put some rocket fuel in her engine. She was somebody he could help and take care of. In the mirror, his face scowled out at him. *Admit it, you'd fall apart without her.*

With clothes on and pockets loaded, he swung through the kitchen to grab whatever caught his eye. Maggie had insisted on filling the fridge with pastries, fruit, cheese, deli meats, drinks and more for everyone. The counter was covered with bread and citrus. A little pride grew in his chest —maybe he wasn't the fucked-up brother anymore.

In the dark early morning, he made his way to each of the properties up for auction, saving his favorite for last. In Rancho Charleston there was an old midcentury modern that had been abandoned for a couple of years.

He parked in the circular driveway in front of the house as the sun rose. The property had been foreclosed and was locked up tight. Through an uncurtained window he could make out parquet floors in the entrance and rippled pink carpet in the living room. A stone wood-burning fireplace took up one wall. It wasn't a house that would be easy to flip but the old neighborhood had charm. Maggie might like it.

In the backyard was an old barn-like structure, listing to one side. It had double bay doors big enough for his large work truck. Through a crack in the door, he could make out the dim interior filled to the ceiling with junk. There was actually a loft.

Something rustled around inside. A minute later, pitiful meowing came from a dark corner. Chase tested the doors and windows but everything was locked up tight—all of it recently tacked down. On the back side of the building was a fresh plywood board covering a hole low on the siding. The cat was trapped inside.

He tried calling the number attached to the listing but was hung up on by a full voice-mailbox. "Hold on, Kitty," he said to the now frantic meowing on the other side of the door. "I won't forget ya."

The auction was attended by many of the usual suspects,

most everyone clutching take-out coffee cups. Chase stepped into the big room, considering where he wanted to stand.

"Hey, Buddy," said old con-man Joe in an overly jovial voice. Joe never missed an auction. "Which one you got your eye on, son?"

"I looked 'em all over a couple times," Chase said, scanning the room for a spot out of Joe's sight.

Joe slapped his paddle against his leg. "That Summerlin property's overpriced. But it's gonna have every dog scratching at the door."

Chase grunted. "Yep. Another one in Tulle Springs was added late."

Joe pulled out his phone. Apparently, the mini mansion added to the list yesterday was news to him. Chase slid away.

The hot properties went fast and high. Joe bought the Summerlin house, a smug smirk on his face. Chase exhaled— maybe the snake wouldn't drive his bid up to be nasty.

The room had thinned out by the time they got to the Rancho Charleston house. He waited until the last moment to raise his paddle. Joe, he noticed, was looking at his phone. Another person upped the bid. Chase raised his a fraction and then they went back and forth as the price creeped up. Sweat trickled down the back of his neck. He raised again.

"Sold," announced the auctioneer. The house was his.

All in all, he'd come out better than he'd expected. He wrote a check for a handful over one hundred thousand and signed the papers. The win sat in his gut like stale bread. These damn auction houses were a potluck of surprises, and he wouldn't even be able to see the interior until the certificate of sale arrived in another ten days.

On the drive back to the Rancho house he stopped at a Quick Mart and bought a bag of cat food and a bowl for water. He'd have to break into the damn shed illegally to help the cat. Hopefully, no one would get their panties in a wad.

Back in the big backyard of the house, he pried off the board low on the siding of the barn-shed. Something had collapsed on the other side and blocked the hole. The cat cried inside. He scratched his chin, sure he didn't have the big bolt cutters he'd need for the chain or padlock.

He went to work with his power screwdriver. The old strap hinges on the door were a pain to unscrew but he got them off. With a creak, he pulled the door away from the barn side. A scrawny gray cat shot out between his legs. He turned on his phone flashlight and shimmied inside through the narrow opening.

A faded and rotten old speed boat blocked much of the floor space, particularly because stuff encapsulated it from floor to two-story ceiling. "Damn." Dust motes swirled around him.

He followed a narrow path further inside toward the rung-ladder access to the second story. High on the pile of junk, bright green eyes caught in the beam of light.

More than one cat, fucking fabulous. Another cat hissed right next to his head, and he stumbled sideways, tripped, and fell into a wall of garbage. The mountain of crap wobbled and came crashing down.

CHAPTER TWENTY-SEVEN

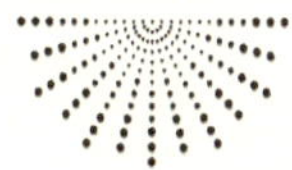

Maggie paced around the house with Toto at her heels. She'd already grilled the chicken kabobs and had them in a pan with foil on top to keep them warm. There was a sports game on the television, with the volume off, and music played from the Bluetooth speakers in the kitchen. The Montgomerys would arrive any minute and Chase was missing.

She checked her phone again. Still nothing. He was late but not heinously so—he always cut his timing too close. Not getting a response from him at all was what had the hair standing up on the nape of her neck.

On a little side table in the family room was a photo of her and Chase that the professional photographer had taken in front of the big fountain downtown. She reached out and touched the silver frame, turning it a little to catch the light.

The doorbell rang. Someone knocked on the door, then the doorbell rang again. Toto lost his mind in a barking frenzy. She put him in the office by the front door. Maggie took a deep breath, smoothing down her vintage Vegas T-shirt.

She opened the door and stared down at a boy bouncing on the balls of his feet. "This is Chase's house, right? Where's the pool? Does your dog bite?" The boy turned around and shouted over his shoulder, "Dad, where are my swimmin' shorts?"

A young woman ran up to the door, carrying a toddler. "Hi," she called, "I'm Ellie and this is Ryder. He popped out of his seat like a shot and ran up here before I could stop him. Sorry—but you are Maggie, right?"

Maggie stepped aside and kept a smile on her face. There were so many of them in the driveway unloading out of two different cars. "Yes, I'm Maggie. Chase is running late. Come on in—there's a ton of food waiting for you in the kitchen."

The boy ran past her into the house. "Really?" Ellie said, a cheerfully excited expression on her face underneath a messy bun of pink hair. The red-haired toddler squirmed out of her mother's arms and ran off after her brother. "Short flight but traveling with the kids is always a circus. Here's Austin. This place is amazing by the way, thank you for having us. Whoops—Ryder opened the back door. I better go and make sure no one drowns. Can't wait to see the pool."

"Hi, I'm Austin," said a very tall blond man wearing a cowboy hat, carrying two suitcases in each hand and three bags strapped over his torso. His eyes scanned past her toward his family, squealing by the pool.

"Maggie," she said. "Come in, I'm really happy to meet you all. Chase isn't back yet but should be here soon."

"Nice place," he said, solemnly.

She told him about the food and pointed out the bedrooms up on the second floor.

Austin nodded, said, "Thank you," and hauled his bags further into the house.

Another cowboy walked up to the door hauling suitcases, but he was grinning at the pretty brunette next to him wearing a dress. He turned his smile on Maggie and she blinked.

"You must be Maggie. Damn, girl, it's about time we met you in person. Don't tell me Chase is still working? This visit might turn into an intervention."

"Hi, I'm Randi. Thank you for hosting."

"This is her first time in Sin City and we're gonna make some bad choices."

Maggie grinned. "It's a good place for that. Lunch is waiting for you inside and Chase should be on his way."

Dolly, Chase's mom, shoulder length silver-blonde hair styled in waves around her smiling face, walked up behind Buck and Randi. They'd spoken a few times over video calls. Dolly had always been very friendly, but Maggie found herself holding her breath.

"Oh, my goodness, darlin', aren't you the cutest thing. Come over here and hug me—you're the hero of the family for sticking with our Chase during his rough patch." Dolly's eyes shone and Maggie blinked as she walked forward into a maternal hug.

"Thank you. You're all so kind—I'm a little overwhelmed but so happy to see you."

Dolly patted her back. "You're doing great. Here's Chip. He doesn't want any help so don't bother offering." Dolly kept an arm around her back as they both stepped to the side to let in a big man using a cane.

"Hi ya, Maggie," Chip said. "Good to meet ya."

The house became a loud chaotic jumble of laughing, shouting children, and conversation. Maggie gave tours, found everyone a room, and eventually showed the kids and Ellie the hot tub. The weather was too chilly for the pool, but she'd warmed up the hot tub enough that the kids could get in there.

The whole time she didn't know if she wanted to be

angry or worried about Chase. She settled on anxious—her gut was telling her something was off. When she could slip away from the crowd, she called Jose.

"Hello?" Jose had answered his phone next to some kind of compressor engine.

"Hey, it's Maggie. Have you seen Chase?" She'd learned to get to the point fast with the contractors.

"What?" He puffed, apparently walking as the sound of the engine got lower. "Chase? Do you know where he is?"

Maggie grabbed her necklace. "No. He was supposed to be here two hours ago. Do you know what happened today at the auction?"

"Uh, no. I think he was going to bid though, right?"

She paced back and forth in their bedroom, her stomach twisting. "He's missing. I think something happened. Call me if you think of anything."

"Shit. Okay—sorry, Maggie, I can't help more. Let me know what happens."

She hung up. Chase had been planning to work with Jose for a couple hours that morning. First, he was headed out to look at his top three auction properties. Her heart pounded. Car accident?

On his laptop she went through everything he'd been doing during the last two days. He'd done a lien search on a property over on Rancho and another in Summerlin. More digging and she had two addresses. She ran downstairs.

In the kitchen, all the adults were chatting, eating, and watching football. She blew out a breath. They'd all be pretty annoyed with her if her hunch was wrong.

She switched the main light on and off. They all pivoted toward her, and conversation stopped. "Everyone, I'm sorry to worry you all, but I have a bad feeling about Chase—he isn't answering his phone. He should have been here hours ago and he's good about staying in touch. I just found out his coworker didn't see him this morning."

Dolly had a hand on her chest. "Oh no."

Maggie swallowed. "I'm going to head out and see if I can find him at one of the properties he set out to look at early today. Maybe he lost his phone or had car trouble…"

Buck stood up and so did Austin. "I'm comin' along," said Buck.

"Yep," said Austin.

Maggie nodded. Driving around the city with them would be uncomfortable but she wouldn't turn down help.

"Could someone here make calls?" She couldn't meet anyone's eyes or else she'd start crying. "It's probably way too early to get news, but the police or hospitals might know something. I'm so sorry—hopefully I'm worrying for no reason."

In the driveway, her minivan was trapped inside the garage by the family's rental cars. She grabbed the keys to the moving truck Chase kept his tools in. She eyed it dubiously—the thing was a beast to drive.

Buck walked up next to her, pulling on a jacket. "We could take one of these little rentals."

"Would be good to have the tools though," said Austin, stepping up beside him.

"I'm insured on the truck, so I better drive," said Maggie, her shoulders tense. "Would you watch me back out?"

On the road she told them about the auction and the properties Chase had gone to look at. "We'll go to the Rancho house first, because I think that's the one he was excited about. He asked me if I like midcentury modern architecture the other day. I said I had no idea. He liked that it was empty and had a big barn in the backyard."

"Probably wants to park this truck in there," said Buck.

"The heat'll peel paint off cars in the summer, without cover," said Austin.

They were crammed into the cab, squeezing in hip to hip on the bench seat. Maggie gripped the steering wheel as she eased the big truck through traffic. "We're close to the strip over here," she muttered.

The house was in an older neighborhood with some big trees and wide sidewalks. Old Vegas, she'd heard this part of town referred to. The houses were mostly one story, and a little funky. It looked like a place she'd like to walk in.

"There's his truck," she yelled. She turned onto a large circular drive in front of a long ranch-style house with a big central gable.

Before she'd fully stopped, she threw the truck into park and then jumped out of the driver's side door. "Chase," she shouted, running over to his truck, which was empty. The house was locked up tight.

"In the barn," Austin called from the side yard.

She sprinted after him. Some tools were spread out on the ground in front of the lopsided old barn, and one of its doors had the hinges unscrewed.

"In here," came a muffled shout and then coughing.

"Chase?" She wrenched at the door, sliding through into darkness as her eyes adjusted.

"Be careful," Chase croaked. "There's shit up to the ceiling that'll fall on you. Maggie, you're gonna need help."

"We're here, brother," said Buck. "You buried in garbage back there?"

"Fucking loft collapsed."

"Are you hurt?" Maggie clicked on her phone's flashlight. She couldn't make sense of what she was seeing for a while. "A bunch of firefighters would get you out of there fast."

"No." Chase coughed some more. "I'm okay, but I'm pinned down and can't crawl out. Lost my phone. Was letting out a damn cat then got curious and snuck in here. Let's save money and trouble and see if you all can get me out."

"We brought your tool truck," Austin called from behind them. "Gonna cut that bolt off so we can move and see. Hang on, Chase."

They ended up taking off both doors because it was faster to unscrew the hinges. Once they could see, the interior was revealed to be a total dumping ground from the floor to the ceiling. Cats stared at them from the shadows. The dust they stirred up as they hauled rotten bags and broken furniture off Chase reeked of urine and mothballs. Austin and Buck had to spend a while propping up the part of the loft that hadn't collapsed with some lumber from the truck.

At last they were able to jack up the beam pinning Chase down. He'd been saved by an old metal shelf that had created a pocket of space for him when part of the loft had fallen. There was a bad moment when more of the second story collapsed but they all managed to jump clear. Back at the jack, Austin and Buck widened the gap enough that Chase pushed himself through.

They stumbled out of the barn, bent over and coughing. Maggie put an arm around Chase's back, her eyes stinging.

"Try calling my phone for me," Chase gasped out. "I could hear it in there. I think you called me a few times, babe."

"Oh my God," she said, hunched over. "I can't believe I almost lost you to a junk barn."

He hugged her. "Thank you for finding me."

His brothers clapped him on the back. Buck found his phone, miraculously. Chase left out cat food and water. He had some cuts, and probably a bruised rib, but otherwise had escaped being crushed by garbage.

"Bought this place," Chase said, hobbling over to sling an arm around her shoulders. "Hell of a deal."

Maggie shook, staring at him with her mouth open.

CHAPTER TWENTY-EIGHT

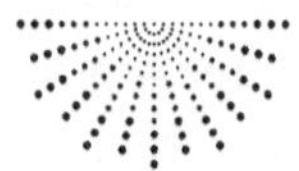

To Maggie, Chase took it all in his stride. He smiled, and cracked jokes, holding her hand, then they limped up to the shower. They were both filthy.

"Come on in here with me," Chase called from the big bathroom attached to their bedroom. "It'd be nice to stand there and let you scrub me down. Damn shoulder aches where the shelf hit me."

It was too much and the dam inside her burst. She walked in, grabbing a tissue to wipe her face.

Chase put one arm around her waist. "You okay?"

She gulped. "No. That was horrible."

He put his head down on top of hers. "Yeah, it was. I was trapped in there for four hours. Kept wondering what the hell MacGyver would do. You never watched those?"

"Why aren't you more freaked out? I would have lost it."

He rolled his shoulders. "Kept telling myself I was lucky. Then I calculated how long it would take you to figure out I was missing and find me. I was spot on."

Her face scrunched up. "I should have looked sooner."

"Nah, you did fine. Come on now, let's get cleaned up."

Once his clothes were off, she realized how much first aid he needed and got to work. There was a deep cut on his forearm and his shoulder and a bunch of scratches on his back. Everything was filthy. One of the shower heads came off the wall and she used it to pretty much pressure wash his skin. He teased her, and wanted to mess around, but she was too worried. She used butterfly bandages on the big cuts because he refused to go in for stitches, insisting they weren't deep enough.

He made it back downstairs to spend a couple of hours with his family. They were a loud bunch, except for Austin, who teased each other and cracked as many jokes as they could find. She didn't know anyone enough to really join in. Did he know how lucky he was to have a family like this? She thought they were a little incredible.

"I think," said Buck, "we're gonna have to leave you behind tonight, brother." He flashed a lopsided grin at Chase. "Although, I'd wheel you around on a cart if you wanted me to."

"Nah," said Chase. "Go on and party. I'm gonna rest up. What about you, Maggie? Head on out if you're feelin' it."

"No, I'll stay home." She leaned against his side. He smiled at her.

"We're taking it easy too," said Dolly. "We'll keep an eye on the kiddos."

"Okay," said Buck, rubbing his hands together. "Let's go spend some money."

Everyone bustled about. Maggie put a casserole into the oven and prepared a salad. The kids ate a quick grilled cheese dinner and were hustled off to bed, the cute three-year-old girl yawning and rubbing her eyes.

Dolly came into the kitchen as Maggie set down the hot food on a trivet on the counter.

"My word, you wrangled this up fast. I thought I had plenty of time to help."

"I've been working in food service since I was fourteen," Maggie said. "This is nothing compared to a solo shift at a diner."

"Thank you." Dolly ran her hands across the countertop. "Maggie, I don't know how to find the right words. Chase is back to himself—I was worried for a long time. I mean it when I say I hope you'll be a part of this family."

Maggie stopped moving. "Really?"

Dolly hugged her firmly, then stepped over to the counter to move the salad bowl. "You're Chase's angel. Sometimes we find our person like that. Chip was in a rough spot too when we met. A rodeo chaser, drinking, brawling. Wouldn't guess it now, would you. Well, people go through rough patches."

Maggie leaned against the counter. "That's so kind of you —really, thank you." She swallowed. "I worry that Chase and I come from different backgrounds. I grew up very poor, Ms. Dolly, raised by my grandmother and step-grandfather. I did well in high school but that's all the education I've had." She forced herself to meet Dolly's eyes. Maybe there was compassion there, she wasn't sure. "Chase met me while I was living in my van, trying to get started on culinary school here in Vegas." She took a deep breath. "He saved me too."

Dolly hugged her again. "I knew I'd raised a good man. I'm glad to hear he helped you—sounds like you and him are about even then. That's balanced."

Maggie stepped back to dab at her eyes with a tissue. "I don't know. But I love him. He really scared me today."

Lucas and his mother showed up then, just in time for Chase's cousin to jump in the car with Buck, Randi, Austin, and Ellie and head down to the strip. Dolly embraced her sister, promising to get her home later and take good care of her all weekend. Chase's aunt was better but still struggling.

Austin's son, Ryder, snuck downstairs to "check on Toto," and then ended up cuddling on his grandmother's lap until he was put back to bed. Chip dozed off in his chair and snored softly, like a rumbling engine.

Maggie petted Toto and sat with Chase's legs in her lap while he leaned back with an ice pack on his bruised rib. She'd needed this, to see Chase with his family. It all made her a little light-headed. How had an impostor like her snuck into this clan?

CHASE GOT TO HIS FEET, none too steadily. "I'm calling it, Ma. Goodnight, Aunt Peggy. See you all in the morning."

Maggie stood up next to him. "I'll head upstairs too. Goodnight and let me know if you need anything."

When he held out his hand, she took it. Toto picked up the stuffed chicken Ryder had given him and trotted ahead of them up the stairs.

"Everyone is so friendly and kind in your family—is that the way they are all the time?"

He cocked his head, trying to work out what she meant. "They have their grumpy moments. But, yeah, they weren't puttin' on a show or anything. My brothers are a couple of whipped puddings now. Used to make me damn jealous. Now I have you though. I'm still hopeful we'll beat them to the altar."

She swung around in the middle of their bedroom and faced him. He closed the door behind him. "You want to one-up your brothers by getting married first?"

He went down on one knee in front of her. "I need you, Maggie. I want to give you the best that I have to offer and move into the next phase of our lives. You anchor me—I've screwed up a lot in the past, I'm a far from perfect man, but

I'm gonna do right by you. You saw me at my worst and still love me. You're special, a fighter, a risk-taker like me, with a moral center I admire. I love you. Will you marry me?" He pulled the ring box out of his pocket and opened it in front of her.

She put a hand over her mouth. "Oh, my word, look at that diamond."

"Want to try it on?"

She reached out shakily and took the box. "You're always moving too fast—I'm not sure I can keep up. But I realized today I'd never recover if I lost you. Actually, I kept thinking what if you were in the hospital and I couldn't even see you because I wasn't family."

"Damn good point."

She huffed, clutching the ring box against her chest, tears running down her face. "Here you are, offering exactly what I want. I haven't said yes because I don't want to take advantage—and because I feel less than, a poor girl that's somehow pulled the wool over your eyes. But, if you want to do this, I'm going to say yes, count my blessings and knock on wood. I'll take it seriously and maybe someday I'll feel worthy of all this fortune. I love you. Yes, I'll marry you."

He rested his head against her belly, wrapping his arms around her waist. "Fucking finally. I booked us a spot at The Little White Chapel for Monday afternoon."

"In two days! Wait, isn't that the one with the drive-up window?"

CHAPTER TWENTY-NINE

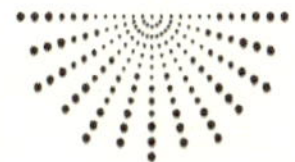

Maggie found herself going along with Chase's plans. She'd never really dreamed of a big wedding—who would she invite? The only people she regretted not having there were the church ladies back in Ridgeview, and her handful of other friends.

"Call them," Chase said when she told him. "We'll plan a trip back to Ridgeview and have a reception party there or whatever you want to cook up, babe."

"What about your work crew?"

His fingers formed a steeple in front of his chest. "Well, they're great guys, and we'll take them out somewhere next week, but keeping it family this weekend makes everything simpler. I have a reservation at Prime Steakhouse with a view of the Bellagio Fountains. Not somewhere we'll eat every week. I thought we'd take everyone to the Stratosphere tomorrow…Hey, why the sad face?"

"You've got everything planned out and it sounds amazing, but I'm not even lifting a finger or making any choices here…"

He hugged her. "You're right. If you'd said yes to me the first time I asked you, we wouldn't be in this bind."

"What bind! Why the rush?"

"Everybody's here. Okay, I'm gonna be real honest with you. I didn't want you to worry about how much everything costs. I booked it all so we'd have the option—a fun, easy day to get the legal stuff out of the way. We can do whatever you want in Ridgeview. You'll be totally in charge of that one. Hell, we can organize a big wedding somewhere if you want to."

She took a deep breath. "No, I don't want to do that. But you're too dang bossy—that's the problem."

He tackled her onto the bed and kissed her. "Still love me?"

"Yeah." She sighed. "I do."

He hadn't planned for everything—specifically, her wedding dress. She ran out of the house the next day to go shop with Andy. She called ahead to the handful of bridal shops open on a Sunday and begged for help.

"What?" Andy clutched his to-go coffee cup against his chest. "You're getting married? Tomorrow?"

"I know. Don't try to talk me out of it or I won't invite you to the lavish steak dinner."

He gulped, his eyebrows pinched together. "Shit, Mags, I hope you know what you're doing."

She gripped her luck necklace. "He's the one with all the money to lose. It's romantic of him, but stupid. The first time he asked me was weeks ago. I held out as long as I could, but the man won't let it go."

"Okay, yeah, when you put it like that—but you hardly know him."

"No, *you* hardly know him. I've met his family, have access to his business banking accounts, and screen his email. He's a total maniac. I think one reason he likes me is he figures I'll put up with him. He's right too." She cackled, emotion bubbling up and overflowing in her chest.

Andy narrowed his eyes at her. "You're really doing this, aren't you?"

"Will you be my witness? You'll be the only one there on my side of the aisle."

He sighed and slung an arm around her shoulder. "Course I will. But all kinds of people would be there to see you married, if you gave them notice. Hell, Mags, tomorrow?"

"I'll be throwing a party in Ridgeview—don't let me forget to invite your mother. And I'm buying you a tux. That's what I'd be doing for a maid of honor, I think. I mean a dress. Come on, I'm gonna throw up if I don't find something to wear soon."

Unbelievably, she found it in the first shop. She knew she didn't have time to be overly picky and aimed for a good fit. She tried on a shorter dress, tea-length, with a sweetheart neckline, constructed of lace and tiny pearls, and stared at herself in the full-length mirror. "I found it," she called out to Andy.

When she stepped out of the dressing room, he put a hand over his mouth. "Wow, Mags."

The salesperson nodded decisively. "Yes. And it'll work without alterations. Don't relax yet, you still need shoes, accessories, undergarments. We have a chance of finding it all if your luck holds."

THAT NIGHT they ate dinner at the Stratosphere, which sat on top of the tallest observation tower in the US, and slowly revolved around. Maggie wore her blue dress again and tried to keep a smile on her face as she fought the feeling that anytime now she'd wake up and be back in her trailer.

"One thousand, one hundred and forty-nine feet," said Chase to their big table. All their houseguests were there along with Lucas and his mother, plus Andy.

"Gets in the way of planes," said Austin.

"It's the Top of the World," said Dolly. "I'm light-headed every time I look out these windows."

"Dad, I wanna go on that roller coaster." Ryder stuck his bottom lip out.

"Over my dead body," Austin muttered.

"You're not big enough yet, bud," said Ellie. "But when you are, I'll go with you." She grinned at him. Austin put a hand over his eyes.

Buck slung an arm around Randi's shoulders. "We've got an announcement, and since we aren't all together too often, we're gonna butt in on your celebration, Chase and Maggie, if you don't mind."

Chase crossed his arms and appeared to be about to say something snide.

"Of course we don't," said Maggie. "I want to hear all the news."

Randi adjusted her glasses. "We're thinking of a May wedding, this year. Hopefully, not too hot or smoky."

"Yep." Buck grinned broadly. "The resort will be done, with water in the pool, and bikes for the trail. RSVP quick, and I'll make sure you have one of the best rooms."

Randi frowned at him. She cleared her throat. "We're going to need help. Buck wants to do it big but we're so remote there's no one to hire. I don't know who's going to drive all that way to see us get married but we're staging it all for professional photography to promote the resort as a prime wedding destination." She huffed. "I'm thinking Vegas looks pretty good—"

"It's going to be fine." Buck grinned.

Everyone congratulated them and made promises to help. After a couple of minutes of preliminary planning talk, Chip banged his beer down on the table a few times and glared around.

"There's plenty of time to worry about the food." He pointed a finger at Austin and Ellie. "What about these two heathens? I'm gettin' too old to wait much longer."

Ellie's face turned a bright pink and a vein started twitching in Austin's forehead. Maggie swallowed, wishing she knew how to help them.

"Well." Ellie played with the cloth napkin in front of her. The red-haired toddler buried her face in Austin's shoulder. "This is as good a time as any, I guess, to share our news."

Austin grunted and covered her hand with his on the table. "I guess. Although Grandpa deserves a time-out for that one."

"Really?" Ryder's eyes were big. "Wait, aren't we gonna tell them about the baby in mama Ellie's tummy?"

Dolly gasped. "Are you sure?"

"Four months." Ellie sighed, then smiled.

"And she finally agreed to marry me," said Austin.

Maggie gripped Chase's hand under the table. She had a family. He winked at her. "First," he whispered in her ear.

CHASE MANAGED to pull off surprise limo rides to the chapel the next day. "Damn, bro, you thought of everything," said Buck as they climbed into the second long white car with all the other men, except Andy. But he didn't really count.

The photographer's assistant, riding with the guys, snapped pictures of them all lounged out in their seats.

Chase unbuttoned his tux jacket and smiled. "I live in the marriage capital of the world; it's rubbed off on me."

"Just admit it, you like this mushy stuff." Buck started handing out shot glasses.

"I'm a simple beast." Chase held up his glass. "All I want is sex, nearly every night and morning of my life."

"Hear! Hear!" they all chorused back.

The Little White Chapel didn't waste any time getting them into the main chapel bedecked with fresh flowers. He'd ordered a bouquet for Maggie and a matching boutonniere for himself. All in all, he was pleased with how little work he'd had to do and how little stress they'd had to deal with. And the photos would be cute too.

When Maggie walked up the aisle, he stood up straighter, swallowing hard. The dress showed off her hourglass figure, her beautiful face a little tense but held high as she tried to keep smiling. Her blonde curls were a pile of ringlets on top of her head. Big blue eyes blinked at him, glistening. She was the most ravishing thing he'd ever seen.

Elvis performed their vows stylishly, and quickly, and before Chase knew it, he was sealing their marriage with a kiss. A flurry of picture-taking followed. He whispered in her ear, "That's it. You're mine now."

"You're the one who's been caught."

"I have another surprise."

"Really?"

"We're staying at the Bellagio tonight. I'm gonna get you tipsy and make things happen."

She kissed him. "All I need is you."

EPILOGUE

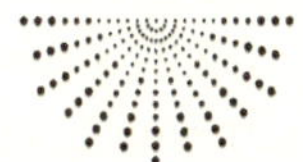

A month and a half later, on a rainy day in March, Maggie was thrown off guard by the packed room for her wedding reception at Ridgeview Presbyterian. Her old boss Darlene had done the catering, and she suspected strong-armed everyone who knew Maggie into showing up.

"We're so happy for you, dear," said Ms. Hazel, a big wobbly smile on her face. "I'm trying not to cry, but I'm not sure I'm going to make it."

"Thank you. I miss you all. If you'd ever like a place to stay in Vegas, call me. I'll fill your room with pastry."

Ms. Hazel patted her face. "I'll do that. Thank goodness you went on your adventure."

She spoke to teachers who had taught her, her ex-boyfriend's parents, coworkers from the diner, and all of her girlfriends who had been able to make it. Carly, who already had two kids, managed to say to her during a break from chasing after toddlers, "Nice job on the hunk. That one looks like a winner. I never did like Todd." She glanced over her shoulder toward where his parents stood on the other side of the room.

The minister said some words and met with them in his office for a little counseling. "I'm proud of you, Maggie," he said, patting her hand. "You're a good person."

Back at the trailer that night, Chase couldn't seem to stop himself from tinkering with this and that while she packed. They'd left Toto boarding at his doggie daycare so that they could fly easily, and because he was still recovering from the corrective surgery on his leg he'd needed for a long time. The trailer didn't seem the same without his scampering feet. It didn't feel like home anymore at all.

"I think I'll sell it," she said, walking back into the kitchen, holding a box packed with old photo albums. She'd ship them and a couple other boxes down to Vegas.

Chase glanced up from where he was reconnecting the drainpipe from the dishwasher. "Not rent it?"

Renting had been her plan. "I'm ready to say goodbye. I used to hope someone would find me here, a distant cousin, something like that." She'd wanted her parents. But her mother had died, and Gran hadn't known anything about her father—someone down in California that had already been married.

She reached up and took down the old iron horseshoe above the door. Her gran had loved her and so had Grandpa Billy. Actually, it turned out the town had thought more of her than she'd thought of herself.

"We can do some online searching for family, if you want," Chase said with his head in the cabinet under the sink.

"Hmm," she mumbled, noncommittally.

Her new life was in Sin City, an optimistic oasis in the middle of deadly desert, where she lived in tank tops and could let her dreams wander. Lately, she'd been imagining her own business, with excellent coffee and long display cases full of beautiful cupcakes.

Chase pulled himself out of the cabinet and stood up,

dusting off his hands. "We'll get a lot done tomorrow. I bet that water heater needs a new T and P valve, then it'll be back in business. Hey, you all right, babe?"

She wrapped her arms around him, pressing her face against his shoulder. "Yep. I just really love you."

The End.

SIGN UP FOR MY AUTHOR
NEWSLETTER

Please help other readers find this book by leaving a review.
Also, receive a free sign-up bonus and learn about new
releases through my author newsletter. You'll hardly hear
from me. Hugs, Anna.

www.annaalkire.com

ACKNOWLEDGMENTS

Biggest thanks to the two best guys in my life, my husband and my son, whose timely hugs and shoulder squeezes have powered my writing life. Love you.

Special heartfelt thanks to my editors and beta readers. Thank you Manda Waller (copyedit), Peter Senftleben (proof), A.M. Vivian (beta), Sam Frontera (beta), and Gennifer Ulmen (beta).

And thank you to the fabulous illustrator, Ashley Santoro, who designed the cover.

FOR A SAMPLE OF ANNA ALKIRE'S
SALLY JONES: A TROPHY WIFE
ROMANCE, TURN TO THE NEXT
PAGE...

Sally Jones: A Trophy Wife Romance

CHAPTER ONE

Does there come a point in every marriage when a woman realizes she might have to kill her husband? As in, if he drops another black sock on the stairs, I'm gonna leave a pillow over his face while he sleeps. You're kidding but it's still the tip of an iceberg.

For me, it hit me like a hammer after I'd been handcuffed to a king-sized bed for three days. Naked as a jaybird. He'd set up security cameras in each corner of that bedroom, that fed into his doomsday-bunker headquarters down the hall.

Josh kicked open the door of the bedroom he'd locked me up in. I flinched, a bead of sweat running down my forehead.

"Hey, baby," he said cheerfully, carrying in yet another bologna sandwich. He stopped at the end of the bed, eyes running over my hunched form as I sat with my arms wrapped around my knees, the long handcuff chain dangling from one wrist. "Mm, you look hot. What you gonna give me for this food?"

Here's the thing. When a rich person loses his mind, all hell breaks loose. Joshua MacCullen, the man I'd married three years ago, had money up every hoo-ha of his oil-slicked family tree. Good fortune rained down on him like manna from heaven. I knew all about his money because I'd been the only one managing it for the last year. Despite looking like an empty-headed blonde with overpriced boobs, I get the sugar sorted with a spreadsheet.

When Josh started staying up all night with his online "friends," buying up guns, and ranting nonsense every time I sat down with him, I spent more time out of the house. We'd always stayed in our own lanes.

"Honey," I said, shrilly. I took a shuddery breath. "We've had a lot of sex, and I know you've been having a good time, but this is a hot mess express." My chin trembled—we'd been over this so many times. "Take this handcuff off me now. It's time for us to move on."

Josh dropped the paper plate on the end of the bed and a can of soda next to it. He was shirtless in the hot June weather, wearing cargo shorts and a loaded gun holster. Cold-blooded. His flat blue eyes stared at me, snake-like.

The meat of the matter was, I'd leave him. And he'd married me without a prenup. I'd been nineteen at the time and about to go back to college after dating him for the summer. He'd taken us to Vegas, to say goodbye, and ended up proposing when we were both horsed, blasted, and tanked. Oh, his daddy had been a flaming ball of righteous rage. My parents had been stunned. Me and Josh, we took off into the sunset, my college plans put on hold.

His pecs flexed on his furry chest. He'd been working out and there was definition on his middle-height frame. His hair patch had fallen off a couple months ago after he'd stopped leaving the house. His bald head shone above the monk ring of hair he had left. I'd thought for the first year of our marriage that he had twelve years on me. He was eighteen years older, now tipping right on into his fortieth year and indulging in a completely unnecessary midlife crisis.

"Can't let you leave, kitten."

"Hon, come on. You know old Mccurty will take good care of you. That lawyer could free the devil himself. Let's back on out of all this trouble. Those people you met online are domestic terrorists—they're gonna end up in jail. It's expensive to fight those charges and they'll clean you out like you wouldn't believe. Turn it all off. Burn that computer. Please, honey. Go walk the holy places—you always talked about doing that."

His eyes shifted away from mine. I held my breath.

He shook his head and stood up straighter. "Hang in there, baby. It won't be long now. Things are happening and we'll be moving on the capital soon." He rubbed his hands together briskly. An alert dinged on his phone. He pulled it out of the holster around his waist, which also had a loaded handgun, and glanced at the screen. "I'll be back real soon."

"No." The catch in my voice turned into a sob. He ignored me, striding through the door and out into the hallway. "Please. I'll make the divorce easy. It won't matter what I want with your lawyers…"

He was gone. I pressed my face against my knees, trying to think through the throbbing in my head as I cried for about the twentieth time since being imprisoned. I'm a patriotic girl, like my whole family. Competing in pageants since I was four years old, I'd given countless speeches about how proud I was and what it all meant. I wanted normal. I'm a practical person, down to my hot-pink manicured toes. And I'm cold-blooded too.

My husband had sunken into a hate-filled vortex of crazy. "Means to an end, baby," he'd said to me when I'd finally made a comment. "There's always a price for power."

Texas had elected a liberal for governor and about half of the population was losing their minds. Josh was planning to shut down the state government and have his followers kill a couple of politicians. He'd found me in his bunker of doom three days ago, figuring out what the hell he was up to, and that's when the shizzle hit the fan.

We lived on a big ranch outside of Austin, Texas, perched up on a hill over Lake Travis, miles away from any other soul and surrounded by forest. He'd picked it out. The sprawling mansion could pass for an old army fort made of stacked tree trunks—just wood every damn place you looked. A few months ago, he'd canceled our landscaping service, and limited the housekeeper to one day a week. She wasn't due for another two days.

People would miss me, my parents most of all. They lived down in Austin and we spent at least one day a week at the country club. I called my mother nearly every day to chat. I stayed busy and I'd had a full week planned with volunteer work and judging at a pageant event. There'd been lunch dates with girlfriends I'd totally stood up. I huffed, my fist clenching. What the hell was I going to say to everybody?

I ate my dry white bread and slab of bologna sandwich and drank from the can. I hated diet soda. Grimacing, I used the five-gallon bucket next to the bed. When I crouched down to set the toilet paper on the floor, I leaned forward and unplugged the bedside lamp. Resisting the urge to look over my shoulder, I pushed the urine bucket toward the open window.

My handcuff had a six foot chain between the two cuffs, one of them locked around my right wrist and the other attached to the wood headboard. I stood up next to the bed and stretched.

The strangest thing was I still cared about him, although it was more like the memory of it, folded up and put in a book. He'd been so cheerful and upbeat for the first two years of our marriage, an easy man to live with. Hadn't cheated on me either, I don't think. He was attentive and sweet in public. He'd been jealous and strange at times in private, but we worked that all out in the bedroom—or so I'd thought. He liked to tie me up and play out his dirty little fantasies. Mild spanking, weird sex toys he'd found, and me ready and willing to spread my legs, bend over, let him tease me endlessly until I was begging for it. What can I say? It worked for us.

Then, about a year ago, my older brother had been visiting my parents and I'd gone out for a night on the town with friends. Josh hadn't felt like going to the bar. Some frisky girlfriends of mine came along, and my brother's best friend, who had grown up next door—Hank Bridger.

I'd always had a crush on Hank. We got drunk together and ended up slow dancing, holding each other close. That, of course, was when Josh found me.

Listen, I refuse to accept any blame for his mental crackup that followed. Sure, I can see that it didn't help things, but I was busting my booty doing everything I could think of to keep the man sane. I took over the finances. Covered for him with family and friends. Kept the ship afloat while he made creepy recordings of himself dressed up like the grim reaper that he shared through YouTube.

I hadn't been stretching long when he stalked back into the bedroom, wearing his fur headdress with long sharp black horns on both sides above his ears. He stuck his chest out, flexing his arms.

"You will call me shaman now," he said.

Flicking my long blonde hair to one side, I crawled onto the bed. He grunted, watching me. I leaned back on my elbows, letting my legs part.

He crawled across the bed, bull-like with those sharp horns on. "There's my girl," he rumbled, pushing my knees wider apart. He nuzzled his face between my thighs, his tongue lashing out at my slit while one of his fingers slid up and pressed into the tight pucker of my bum. I groaned.

"I like you dirty like this," he growled while I squirmed and his finger pressed in harder. "Tonight's going to be special. It's going to hurt, baby. But you're going to want it. I'll make sure you never forget me."

"No, hon, come on now. Please don't—I know you're a good man."

He bit me, hard, and I screamed.

"It's shaman."

"Yep, okay, shaman."

He grunted and went back to his sucking and licking. I started to fake a monster orgasm, squealing and moaning, whispering, "Yes, shaman," while my hand went up to grab my hair then slid sideways like I was reaching for a grip on the headboard while overcome with passion. My heart beat hard enough to explode in my tight chest—if I screwed this up, he would hurt me. Something had shifted and he wasn't the Josh I recognized. I'd have one second after I lunged to the right. My hands shook.

There wasn't any more time to dither. I threw myself sideways and grabbed the lamp, nearly knocking it off the table but I managed to get a hand around the spindle body. His mouth lifted away from me and my stomach compressed. My arm whooshed through the air and I didn't slow down or stop to look at his face. I smashed the brass base of the lamp down hard onto the top of his head, right between the horns.

Sally Jones: A Trophy Wife Romance

PRAISE FOR ANNA ALKIRE

YES!!!! Absolutely amazing story. Addictive, exciting, detailed story. Great characters. Read in one sitting. Way better than five stars.

— LISA PICCIANO

This is not your typical love story and that's a good thing. I happen by this author and book by accident and am so glad I did. Not your average story with so many different possibilities. I couldn't put it down. Will have to find more by this author.

— TRACY E HOGAN

From the very first sentence, this book had me hooked straight away.

— READINGFORTHELOVEOFBOOKS

BOOKS BY ANNA ALKIRE

Buck Up, Buttercup: Montgomery Brothers Book 1

Signs of Trouble: Montgomery Brothers Book 2

Both Fingers Crossed: Montgomery Brothers Book 3

Sally Jones: A Trophy Wife Romance

Somewhere Beyond the Sea: A Trophy Wife Romance

A Gnome Inheritance: A Smitten in Seattle Romance

ABOUT THE AUTHOR

Anna lives in Washington state where she writes, reads, and sews every minute she can. Find out more about her (and grab a free story) at her website.

www.annaalkire.com